NNNNN

Also by Carl Reiner
in Large Print:

My Anecdotal Life

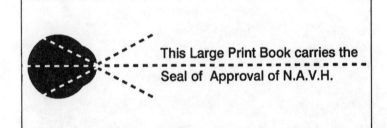

NNNNN

Carl Reiner

Thorndike Press • Waterville, Maine

Published in 2006 by arrangement with Simon & Schuster, Inc.

Thorndike Press® Large Print Americana.

The tree indicium is a trademark of Thorndike Press.

The text of this Large Print edition is unabridged.
Other aspects of the book may vary from the original edition.

Set in 16 pt. Plantin by Christina S. Huff.

Printed in the United States on permanent paper.

Library of Congress Cataloging-in-Publication Data

Reiner, Carl, 1922–
    NNNNN / by Carl Reiner.
        p. cm. — (Thorndike Press large print Americana)
    ISBN 0-7862-8592-3 (lg. print : hc : alk. paper)
    1. Authors — Fiction.   2. Writer's block — Fiction.
 3. Identity (Psychology) — Fiction.   4. Large type books.
 I. Title.   II. Thorndike Press large print Americana series.
 PS3568.E4863N59 2006b
    813´.54—dc22   2006004730

For Estelle

Thank you, George Shapiro, Dan Strone,
Bess Scher, Ruth Fecych, Sybil Pincus

As the Founder/CEO of NAVH, the only national health agency solely devoted to those who, although not totally blind, have an eye disease which could lead to serious visual impairment, I am pleased to recognize Thorndike Press* as one of the leading publishers in the large print field.

Founded in 1954 in San Francisco to prepare large print textbooks for partially seeing children, NAVH became the pioneer and standard setting agency in the preparation of large type.

Today, those publishers who meet our standards carry the prestigious "Seal of Approval" indicating high quality large print. We are delighted that Thorndike Press is one of the publishers whose titles meet these standards. We are also pleased to recognize the significant contribution Thorndike Press is making in this important and growing field.

Lorraine H. Marchi, L.H.D.
Founder/CEO
NAVH

* Thorndike Press encompasses the following imprints: Thorndike, Wheeler, Walker and Large Print Press.

1

AM EPM AGP

(an eon ago)

"My dear brother, I cannot believe what thou art telling me."

"I did see her!"

"Art thou certain it was not our mother thou didst see?"

"It was not our mother!"

"But thou hath said that she had the look of Mama."

"In that she had large breasts and no penis or testicles."

"Thou hath described Mama."

"No, she hath skin darker than Mama's."

"Cain, thou dost not wish to lie with Mama, dost thou?"

"I do not, Abel!"

"Dada said thou must — if thou art to multiply."

"Then I choose not to multiply."

"Cain, where didst thou see this creature?"

"On the other side of the steep hill, lap-ping water from a stream."

"Cain, we are forbidden to leave our garden. Why hath thou disobeyed Dada?"

"To find what lies outside of Eden. And there I did see her. I thought it was Mama and that she had been rolling in mud."

"Mama enjoys to roll in mud —"

"But when I called 'Mama,' she ran off on legs that were thinner and longer than are Mama's. It was the dark woman!"

"It was Mama!"

"Abel, my penis erected! That hath ne'er happened whilst looking at Mama! This morning she drank again from the stream — and, in the sunlight, I could see no mud on her dark skin."

"Cain," Abel scolded, "there are but four humans in the world — and they are all of one color! That is a known fact, a universal truth!"

"And now, Abel, with my new-known fact, we have a new universal truth! There are more than four humans in the world and, the dark woman did say, many more than four."

"And, Cain," Abel scoffed, "how many more does this dark creature, who does not exist, say there are in the world?"

"Nineteen."

"Nineteen? I know of no such word."

"Nor did I — until she showed me nineteen!" Cain said, opening his hand to show many shiny black stones. "See," Cain explained, placing four stones on the ground, "this is how many humans are in our Garden, and here" — Cain placed the remaining agates in Abel's hand — "is how many more there are in the world."

"I see stones," Abel said. "I do not see humans."

"Thou art pigheaded," Cain roared. "Canst thou not accept that one of the stones in thy hand represents one human?"

"I could, if there were a human to be represented by it."

"There is!" Cain shouted, grabbing a stone from his brother's hand. "This is that human woman and I did see her!"

"Does this stone," Abel said, smirking, "have a name?"

"I know it not, but I will learn it," Cain said, caressing the stone, "and I will find her!"

"Thou hath seen no person," Abel argued. "You dreamed her!"

"Did I dream these?" Cain shouted, displaying the stones.

"Thou didst gather them while asleep. I have seen thee walk, talk, and pee in thy

9

sleep! Cain, did thou inform Dada of this dark woman?"

"No, Dada thinks that there are but four of us in the world."

"Dada does not think!" Abel shouted. "Dada knows!"

"Does Dada know from whence we came?"

"From Mama's vagina. Dada told thee."

"Abel, I know not because Dada told me but because I didst see thee come out of Mama — but from whence did Mama come?"

"From Dada's rib," Abel insisted. "Dada hath told us many times."

"And I do not believe it, because I did not see Mama come from Dada's rib."

"So, from whence dost thou think Mama came?"

"I do not know — and didst thou not wonder who made Dada?"

"No, Cain. Dada made himself from his own rib — Dada is a self-made man — he hath told thee that."

"Did Dada tell thee how he did arrive in the Garden?"

Abel smirked again. "Cain, Dada did not have to arrive in the Garden, for Dada was already here!"

Cain sighed and ran off toward the hill.

"Cain, where goest thou?"

"To find her and ask her name," Cain shouted, holding the stone aloft, "and to ask if she will lie with me!"

"She doth not exist, Cain, she is but a dream —"

"Yes, a dream, and she doth exist!" Cain shouted, his voice trailing as he fled the Garden of Eden. "She exiiiiists — she exiiiiiisttttttssss!!"

"That is page four," Nat Noland mumbled as he checked the page count on his computer screen. "Good start," he said, smiling. "Twenty more and we can title this baby!" Experience told Nat that if he wrote twenty-four acceptable pages, a full novel would follow.

N (for "novel") had been the working title of his first novel, *NN* his second, and this being his fifth, Nat typed *NNNNN* into the computer. Being borderline superstitious, and aware that his first published novel, *Normal*, started with an *N* and had been a minor success, he decided that all of his titles would contain a word that began with an *N*.

"You know something, Nat my boy," he told himself, looking at the five *N*'s atop the page, "*NNNNN* could be the title."

11

"Yeah, it has an element of mystery," Nat agreed, "like *M*, that classic German film by Fritz Lang!"

"With Peter Lorre," Nat added excitedly. "One of the all-time great titles — that single letter *M* was intriguing."

"Five *N*'s would be five times as intriguing," Nat said. "Could I justify using all five?"

"Five *N*'s?" Nat whined. "I don't think so."

"How about *No, No, No, No, Nanette!*"

"That was the title of a musical, schmucko!"

"That was *No No Nanette!*" Nat joked. "This has three more 'nos' — and don't call me schmucko!"

"Hey, about this book," he said, grimacing. "Do I really want to do my version of Genesis?"

"That was the idea."

"A little blasphemous, don't you think?"

"A little blasphemy is good — it's provocative — and provocative sells!"

"Not always!"

"Nat, darling," said a soft soprano voice wafting down the stairwell, "you're talking to yourself again."

"Oh, damn! Really?"

"Really, and rather loudly," Glennie answered, balancing a mug on a small tray. "Weren't you aware of it?"

"I'm not sure — I think I was. Shit no, I wasn't! Glennie, could you hear what I was saying?"

"Something about blasphemy," she said, making her way down the stairs, "and you told yourself not to call you schmucko."

"Oh, boy."

"I'm sorry, darling," she said, setting the tray down, "but you did want me to tell you when you're having these conversations."

"Yes, yes! Damn! I thought I was thinking those things. Glennie, I'm getting to be a weirdo."

"Darling, lots of people talk to themselves."

"Yeah, and whenever I see one, I say to myself, 'There goes a weirdo!' I hope I'm saying it to myself. Did you ever hear me say that?"

"Never! Drink your Postum, darling — while it's hot!"

"You know," Nat announced, picking up the oversize mug, "a lot of people think I'm weird for drinking Postum."

"I drink it."

"Yeah, but you don't talk to yourself," he said, sipping from his mug. "I am definitely a weirdo — I'm even writing weirdly."

"How is your novel coming, darling?" she asked brightly, hoping to buoy his spirits.

"It's not," he said, taking two short sips.

"Not coming?"

"It's coming, but I'm not sure it's a novel!"

"What is it, then?"

"I don't know, but whatever it is, it's flying out of me. I know one thing, though: It's going to disappoint my publisher and the people he likes to call my 'loyal readers.' "

"Nat, would you like me to read it?"

"No, it's only four pages — and I don't need you to be disappointed too."

"I have a feeling I won't be, but if you think —"

"I do! It's like nothing I've ever written — the subject, the style — the font —"

"The font?"

"Yeah, instead of Times New Roman, I'm using Monotype Corsiva. Never used that before — crazy, huh?"

"Monotype Corsiva? No, that's wonderful, darling!" Glennie gushed, clueless as to what Monotype Corsiva looked like. "You *have* been grousing about repeating yourself."

"No, Glennie, it was the critics who were grousing about that."

"But you didn't disagree."

"No, I didn't. Hey, Glennie, those times when I talk to myself," he asked worriedly, "do I always answer myself?"

"Very often, and lately, sweetheart — you've been using a different voice."

"How's it different?"

"Well, it's deeper and kind of whiny."

"Really? Hmm, deep-voiced men usually don't whine."

"Well, your guy does. The first time I heard that voice was at my brother's birthday party. You were in the powder room arguing, and I thought there was someone with you. I knocked and asked if you were alone, and you said, 'I am never alone.' Do you remember that?"

Nat's face darkened. He repeated the line as he stirred his Postum and stared at the coffee-colored vortex. "Yes, Glennie," he said, nodding, "I do remember."

"What did you mean, 'I am never alone'?"

"I don't know — what did you think I meant?"

"I thought you'd found a clever way to tell me not to pester you."

"No, that's not it," he said, closing his eyes and mouthing the words. "I am never alone —"

"Are you all right, darling?" Glennie asked softly.

"No, I am definitely not all right."

"Is there something I can do?"

"There might be" — he sighed and looked at her beseechingly — "if you can remember that young doctor's name — the one your friend Jane was rhapsodizing about at dinner last month."

"Oh, yes," Glennie said, pleased at his interest, "a reputedly brilliant Viennese psychoanalyst."

"Yes — had a strange name," Nat offered, "like — uh, Dr. Fruit!"

"I think Jane said Dr. Frucht."

"Frucht! That's right! *Frucht* in German means 'fruit,' " Nat added excitedly. "How do I get in touch with him?"

"Well, I jotted down his name — in case. Uh, darling, are you thinking about making an appointment with this psychiatrist?" she asked innocently.

"Glennie, are you worried about a shrink tampering with the psyche of someone you once described as — *my perfect husband?*"

"A bit," she lied.

"But if he finds a way to make me more perfect, you wouldn't object?"

"Not for a moment, dear."

2

"If this Dr. Frucht is such a hotshot," Nat asked himself impatiently, waiting for the light to change, "how come he answers his own phone?"

"Because psychiatrists don't have secretaries," he offered. "I think to guard against a breach of confidentiality."

"Well, why was it so easy to get an appointment?" Nat shot back. "Do you really believe that his two o'clock patient canceled to give birth?"

"I do. Why would he make that up?"

The moment the light turned green, Nat stepped on the accelerator and swerved sharply to avoid hitting a car that had darted in front of him.

"Hey, asshole!" Nat shouted. "You don't turn left from the right lane!"

"Whoa, he's an eighty-year-old asshole," Nat calmly pointed out. "Forty years from now, that could be you!"

"They should revoke his license!" he whined, gunning the motor.

"Hey, are you trying to kill me?"

"Do you want to drive?" Nat lifted his hands from the wheel.

"I had better," he snapped, grabbing the wheel, "if you're serious about seeing the great Dr. Frucht."

Stopping at another red light, Nat wondered if he had been giving voice to his thoughts. He flipped down the visor to check his image in the mirror.

"If this Dr. Frucht is so great, why is his office in Tarzana and not Beverly Hills?"

Nat was upset to see his lips moving and hear words coming from them.

Dr. Frucht had set up shop in a new three-story commercial building. The sparse listing in the lobby directory suggested that suites were available.

Nat Noland never passed up an opportunity to check lobby directories for unusual names. Nadesjda, the heroine of his best-reviewed novel, was a name he had cadged from a doctor of internal medicine, Nadesjda Shlocht. To avoid a lawsuit, he had changed Nadesjda's last name to Smythe. Nat happily noted that this directory sported an unusually high percentage of exotic names. Besides Dr. Frederich Frucht, there was a Dr. Phillip A. Druul, Orthodontist, and an R. G.

Neparia, Physical Therapist.

"Neparia," he mumbled, jotting it in his notepad. "That's a keeper."

"And how about this one: Dr. Jertrude Trampleasure, Ph.D.?"

"Hmm, Jertrude, with a *j* — definitely worth noting," Nat said, scribbling "Jertrude" on his pad.

"How about Trampleasure?" he asked himself.

"No — name sounds made up."

"Sir, I think you will find that all names are *made up!*" a vigorous, British-accented female voice instructed. "Trampleasure was *made up* in the eleventh century by one of my paternal forebears."

Nat turned and faced a smiling, uncommonly attractive redheaded woman.

"Oh, I am so sorry," he sputtered. "I didn't realize that I was — uh —"

"Talking to yourself?" Dr. Trampleasure asked good-naturedly.

"Well, yes. I do apologize. I love unusual names, and both of yours are that."

"Well, I grant that there are not many Trampleasures in this country," she said, pushing the elevator button, "but you do have your fair share of Gertrudes."

"You pronounce it Gertrude, with a hard *g?*"

19

"Yes, don't you?" she asked, amused.

"Well, I would say Jertrude, with a soft *g* — as in George."

"And why would you?"

"Because" — he shrugged, pointing to the directory — "you spell it with a *j*."

"I do not!" the doctor insisted, checking the directory. "But obviously the keeper of the directory does. Heads will roll!" She laughed. "How stupid of me. I've been a tenant for two days now, and I hadn't thought to check. Thank you for bringing it to my attention."

"You're welcome, Dr. Trampleasure. I guess talking to oneself out loud has its positive aspects."

As they rode up in the elevator, Nat introduced himself and explained why he collected interesting names. Dr. Trampleasure allowed that she might enjoy reading about a heroine named Jertrude if her last name weren't Trampleasure.

Nat and the doctor alighted at the same floor and found themselves going down the corridor together and stopping at offices that were directly across the hall from each other. As she unlocked her door, she turned and stared at Nat.

"Mr. Noland, have we ever met before?"

"I doubt it," he said. "I would remember

20

you — and your name!"

"I'm sure you're right," she said, "but I have this strange feeling that I know you from somewhere — but no matter — lovely to have met you."

Nat waited for her to enter her office before mumbling, "Now, that is one charming woman."

"With beautiful teeth," he agreed.

"And a Ph.D."

"And she thinks she knows me. Maybe I should go see her."

"First let's see what Dr. Frucht has to offer."

"Except for what Janie Wells told us," Nat said, entering the dimly lit waiting room, "what do I know about this guy?"

"Well, I know that he probably has no obese patients," he mumbled as he sat down on a fragile-looking cherrywood settee. "Hmm, *National Geographic*," Nat said, glancing at the magazine rack, "gave me my first look at bare breasts."

"The first *long* look," he argued, unaware that Dr. Frucht had emerged from his office. "You saw cousin Deeana's tits first."

"Right. At the beach house," Nat concurred, "and Mom got mad when she heard me comparing the size of Deeana's tits to Lenny's sister's."

21

On hearing two deliberately enunciated "ahems," Nat stopped reminiscing.

"I am Dr. Frucht," the doctor announced, rolling the *r* in Frucht, "and you are Mr. Nat Noland?"

"Yes, I have an appointment," Nat offered gratuitously. "I — I was talking to myself, wasn't I?"

"I believe you were," the doctor answered. "Please come in."

"What did you hear?" Nat asked, entering the office.

"A discussion about tits — comparing the size of your cousin Dinah's and —"

"Deeana's," Nat corrected.

"Yes, Deeana," the doctor said with a nod, shutting the door. "Please to have a seat."

The chair facing the doctor's desk was as flimsy as the waiting-room settee. A more substantial-looking wicker couch was available, but Nat ruled it out.

No sir, he thought, *I'm not ready to lie down and spill my guts out to this Freudian-bearded shrimp.*

Dr. Frucht was a small, neat man with a narrow face and a full head of downy mouse-colored hair.

The man looks like a kiwi, Nat thought. *How can I trust someone whose name means fruit and who looks like a fruit?*

22

Checking the decor, Nat divined that Dr. Frucht was partial to brown. His desk, suit, tie, and the Rembrandt print he had behind his desk were all shades of brown that blended beautifully with the textured wallpaper. Nat watched with interest as the doctor picked up a pitcher of water and filled two stemmed glasses.

The man is gay! he thought.

"What are you thinking, Mr. Noland?"

"That you were gay—*ing* to," Nat blurted out, "*go*—ing to offer me water."

"Yes, would you like some?" He offered Nat a glass.

"Thank you," Nat said, gulping down the entire four ounces, hoping that his faux pas had gone unnoticed.

If he's any kind of analyst, Nat thought, *he had to have caught my attempt to cover up "gay-ing" with "go-ing."*

"Let me refill that for you," the doctor said, taking Nat's glass. "These do not hold much. I ordered some ten-ounce tumblers that should be delivered today. By the way, I am not gay."

"Huh?" Nat asked, his glass poised at his lips.

"You were wondering if I was gay, weren't you?" The doctor handed back the refilled glass.

"Was I?" Nat said, gulping water.

Sonovabitch, Nat thought, *the man is perceptive.*

"You asked me if I was *gay*-ing to offer you water," the doctor explained good-naturedly.

"Yes, I did. I'm sorry, Doctor —"

"Don't give it a thought. Most people assume I am homosexual."

"Is that right? Well," Nat added quickly, "it doesn't matter to me."

"It would not matter to you if I were gay?"

"Not at all," Nat said forcefully. "I have quite a few gay friends — really good friends — *really* gay ones. Do you know Carson Lamply? You probably don't — he was my lit professor in college and a great influence on me — and he was a homosexual — still *is* — we keep in touch — not as often as either of us would like but we do keep in touch — Christmas cards — never missed a year —"

Nat was aware that he was rambling but could not stop.

"I send him all my novels and Carson sends me his essays and anything he thinks would interest me. Whoa, Nattie boy," he admonished himself, "you are going on a bit too long about a subject you say you're comfortable with. Pretty significant, huh, Doctor?"

"It may be," Dr. Frucht responded. "So, tell me, Mr. Noland, what brings you to my office?"

"Well, this is going to sound a little crazy to you — or maybe not — I'm sure you've heard crazier. Say, Doctor, without giving names, what's the craziest reason a patient had for coming to see you? Whatever it is, I'll bet mine takes the cake."

"Mr. Noland," the doctor asked patiently, "why are you here?"

"You heard why — in your waiting room — I talk to myself."

"Many people talk to themselves."

"But I have long conversations — and my wife says that lately I've been talking more often — and louder. What troubles both of us is that I'm not aware that I am."

"You are not aware," Dr. Frucht asked, his eyebrows subtly arching, "that you are talking aloud?"

"That's right, Doctor! I take the cake, don't I?"

"Do you ever know when you are talking to yourself?"

"I guess not. In your waiting room, when you interrupted my conversation with your aheming, I had no idea. Pretty crazy, eh?"

The doctor delivered a generic "hmm," closed his eyes, and tilted his head back.

Now, that's pretty crazy, Nat thought. *He's staring at the ceiling through closed eyelids.*

Dr. Frucht remained silent and motionless for what seemed to Nat much longer than the ten seconds it was. The silence was broken by two voices speaking simultaneously. Nat asked, "Should I tell you a little about myself?" and the doctor said, "Why don't you tell me about yourself."

Their answers overlapped, Nat saying "Okay," the doctor saying "Yes, tell me about yourself."

Nat Noland took a deep breath and, for thirty-five minutes, described his childhood in some detail, insisting that "it was a relatively happy one."

Dr. Frucht listened attentively until ten minutes before the session was scheduled to end, when he leaned forward and uttered an enunciated "a-hem," signaling Nat to stop talking. A frustrated Nat could not stop. He had just begun to recount how, in high school, his heart had been permanently damaged by the breathtakingly beautiful Helen Melonsky.

"The jocks referred to her as Helen Melons," Nat rattled on. "Every guy in the school was in love with her — she didn't know I existed — it wasn't until my junior year that I got up the courage to speak to her — we were in study hall —"

"I do want to hear about Helen Melonsky," Dr. Frucht interrupted, "but for today, it would be helpful if you clarify something for me. You said that you were relatively happy as a child. What did you mean by 'relatively'?"

"Well, I did have a baby sister, but only for a few weeks. It was that sudden death thing — I was about a year and a half at the time and I don't remember her at all. I think her name was Nellie — did I tell you that she was also adopted?"

"*Also,* Mr. Noland? *You* were adopted?"

"Oh, yes. I mentioned that, didn't I?"

Dr. Frucht shook his head.

"Oh, I thought I did when I spoke of my parents — are you sure I didn't mention —"

"I am sure that you did not."

"Well," Nat continued animatedly, "they're wonderful people. Jed and Bertha Noland. I couldn't have asked for better parents. I know psychiatrists expect patients to bad-mouth their parents, but try as you may, Doctor, you won't get me to say a negative thing about either one of them. I love my folks and they love me — at least that's what we keep telling each other." Nat laughed. "Is that something I should worry about?"

Dr. Frucht was about to speak when a small red light atop his desk started to blink. The doctor clicked it off, smiled benignly, and informed Nat that the session was over.

"Why did I say yes so fast when he suggested that we meet again next week?" Nat asked himself as he slid his credit card into the self-service gas pump.

"Because Dr. Frucht was on the verge of saying something significant when we ran out of time."

"Which we wouldn't have if you hadn't used so much of it talking about your gay friend Carson Lamply."

"I didn't want him to think I'm homophobic — should I cancel next week's appointment?"

"Let's think about it."

As he filled his gas tank, Nat thought about the doctor and how intently he had listened when Nat spoke of his dead adopted sibling.

"I was sure I told him that I was adopted."

"I know you didn't," he shot back, "because I was about to mention it but I interrupted myself by telling him how some nights I drive Glennie crazy by insisting that we sleep on each other's side of the bed."

"Did you notice how his eyes popped

open when you said how you enjoyed *bed-side swapping* with your wife?"

"Yes, and did you notice how perfectly his eyes matched his necktie?"

"He's weird," Nat concluded, "but so am I — maybe we can help each other."

That evening, after Nat decided he wasn't hungry, he soaked silently for the better part of an hour in the hot bath that Glennie had drawn for him. At one point, in an effort to lighten her husband's mood, she brought in the half bottle of merlot that was left over from Saturday night's dinner. Glennie took some good-natured abuse from friends for her boorish practice of refrigerating leftover red wine and then drinking it instead of using it for cooking. She emptied the chilled merlot into two glasses, giving Nat the lion's share. When asked why the uneven distribution, she quipped, "Darling, you're drinking for two." As the words left her mouth, she regretted them. She had never before been flippant about his problem.

"I'm sorry, Nat, that was mean of me."

"Yes," he agreed, "but it was funny-mean, not mean-mean."

Nat met her further attempts to apologize with assurances that he was not angry and did love and appreciate her. He picked up

29

his glass, toasted their marriage, and announced that he was going to work on his novel.

"I'm guessing, darling, that you don't want to talk about your meeting with Dr. Frucht."

"I will when I figure out what the meeting was about," he said, rising from the tub, pulling on his terry cloth robe, and striding resolutely to his office.

He fired up his computer, put on his glasses, and quickly scanned the pages.

"Whaddya think?" he asked.

"Well, Nattie, in four pages we've got a good mix of incest and blasphemy — and it's all in questionable taste."

"So far, so good!"

"Should we continue writing or get something to eat?"

"Both. I'll write and you go make sandwiches."

"Deal!" Nat said, getting up and starting for the stairs. When he looked back, he was upset to see no one at the computer.

"Well, do we have any doubts about keeping my next appointment with Dr. Fruit?" he asked.

"No, you have just dispelled them!" he agreed, returning to his desk and clicking on the intercom.

"Glennie, sweetie," Nat sang, "would you be a doll and whip up one of your award-winning melted cheese sandwiches?"

Glennie winced when she heard Nat's whiny voice add, "Could you make that two?"

He speaks with two voices, she reasoned, *but he eats for one.*

Glennie made one sandwich and held it hostage until Nat promised to make regular appointments with his psychiatrist.

Nat reached for the sandwich that Glennie left on his desk but stopped to check something he had written on his notepad.

"Hey, how about we name the dark woman Neparia?"

"Neparia, hmm, not too bad. Does it sound biblical?"

"Biblical enough! And it starts with an *n!*"

"How does Cain learn her name is Neparia?"

"I got an idea. Start typing!"

OUTSIDE EDEN

Cain raced up and down steep hills shouting "Neparia," the name that had come to him in a dream.

"Nepariaa, Nepariaaaa," he shouted, but to no avail.

Cain, an impatient man, would ordinarily have felt frustration but instead was exhilarated. Knowing that Neparia existed was enough to keep him smiling, searching, and shouting. In all his life, he had shouted only the name Abel. The one time he'd shouted "Eve!," Adam delivered a blistering lecture on parental respect and sharp blows to his head.

Though there was no response, Cain continued to call her name until night fell. Exhausted, he made his way to the stream.

Neparia will return, *he reasoned,* either thirsting for water — or, hopefully, for the man who calls Nepariaaaaa.

While lying on his stomach and scooping water into his mouth, Cain felt a foot step heavily upon his buttocks. He hoped it was Neparia's foot but knew better upon hearing a rumbling voice ask, "Art thou he who didst call my sister's name?"

"Thy sister's name is — Neparia?" a bewildered Cain did ask.

"Yes. And how knowest thou this?"

"It didst come to me in a reverie."

"And hast thou come to lie atop my sister and make swell her belly?"

"Oh, great is my desire to lie atop your sister and make swell her belly!" Cain shouted eagerly.

"Not to slaughter and butcher her?"

"Why wouldst I slaughter and butcher her?" Cain shuddered.

"To eat of her flesh!" the man growled.

"Eat of her flesh?" an appalled Cain shouted. "Who does such a thing?"

"They who live in the great forest do such things. My brothers, Agu, Moti, and Luca, journeyed to the great forest in search of berries, and Luca did witness Agu and Moti being slaughtered and devoured by the flesh eaters. Hath thee never eaten of the flesh of humans?"

"Never! It mattereth not how hungry we were — Mama, Dada, and Abel never thought to eat of each other."

"What dost thou eat?" the voice demanded.

"Figs, berries, roots, nuts, some flowers — and, when unobserved, an apple."

"And how do they call thee?" a mellowing voice asked.

"I am called Cain."

"And I am called Slama!" the man said, lifting his foot from Cain's back. He smiled, then uttered the most beautiful words Cain had e'er heard spoken: "In time, Cain, thou wilt lie atop my sister, Neparia, and make swell her belly!"

An ecstatic Cain spun around, kissed

Slama's huge foot, and did espy Neparia peeking out from behind a eucalyptus tree.

"Nattie boy, do you know where this is going?"

"I don't have a clue."

"Maybe I ought to take another peek at Genesis?"

"And what? Be influenced by some hack writers who lived thousands of years ago and didn't know their cocks from their coccyx?"

"Or what causes thunder and lightning?"

"Exactly. I may be a hack, but I'm a hack who's had five thousand years of scientific discoveries available to me — discoveries that those ancient scribes never dreamed possible."

Nat took three angry bites of the now congealed melted cheese sandwich before he resumed typing.

When Neparia saw Cain running toward her, she smiled and ran from him. A confused Cain looked to Slama for help.

"Why does Neparia run from me? Does she fear I will eat her? I want but to lie with her and make swell her belly."

"Cain, she runs from thee," Slama explained, "because she may not lie with thee

until thou proveth thyself to be a man Twice Worthy."

"Twice worthy?" asked a confused Cain.

"Twice Worthy!" Slama boomed, his voice echoing in Cain's head. "TWICE WORTHY!"

"What the hell does *Twice Worthy* mean?"

"I don't know — it sounds good."

"It sounds full of shit. I say take it out!"

"I say leave it in!"

"Screw you!"

"Fuck you! I'm going to bed!"

"Do what you want. I'm writing!"

Nat did not go to bed and he did not continue writing. He ate the rest of the cheese sandwich and thought of Glennie and his fear of making swell her belly.

3

London

It was unlike Morton Quigley to leave his flat without an umbrella, especially when his wife, Sarah, and the BBC's weatherman concurred that rain was imminent. For six consecutive days, London had been bathed in brilliant sunlight, and Morton, who enjoyed the twenty-minute stroll to and from his office, wishfully thought that the unseasonable weather would continue, and it did until he was halfway home. As he hugged the buildings trying to avoid the thick sheets of water cascading down, he could hear Sarah imploring him not to be late for their dinner party. After looking about fruitlessly for a cab, Morton sought refuge under the awning of an intriguingly named second-hand bookshop.

* BROWSE 'n' STEEP *
DO BROWSE AMONG OUR BOOKS
WHILE WE STEEP YOUR TEA!

To the chilled, rain-soaked Morton Quigley, a cup of hot tea sounded irresistible. The sound of the friendly tinkle-bell announcing his entrance, and the warmth with which he was greeted by a jolly stout man, made him smile.

"Here, blot yourself, my waterlogged friend," the stout man said, handing him a paper towel. "I'm Mr. Browse, and yes, Browse *is* my real name, Winston Hobson Browse!"

"Mr. Browse." Morton nodded. "And is there a Mr. Steep?"

"Oh, indeed there is. James A. Steep. He is in the back *steeping!* Sir, have you visited our shop before? You do look familiar."

"I have that kind of face. People are always mistaking me for someone else."

"Oh, ho!" Browse laughed. "Steep and I know how that is. Through the years we've often been told we look like Laurel and Hardy. Sadly, each passing year the number of people who remember Laurel and Hardy is diminishing. Do you have time for a nice cup of Mr. Steep's tea, Mr., uh —"

"Quigley, Morton Quigley. Actually, I do not have time, but," Morton added conspiratorially, "for a nice cup of Mr. Steep's tea, I will make time."

Soon Morton Quigley was sipping an exquisitely brewed cup of jasmine tea and telling Browse and Steep how much they did resemble Laurel and Hardy.

"We enjoy hearing that," Mr. Steep said, beaming. "And you enjoy your tea."

"And your browsing!" said Mr. Browse as he left to greet another customer.

Aware that he would have to face an exasperated wife, Morton snaked his way through long rows of secondhand books, looking for a peace offering. Sarah, a voracious reader of romance novels, had read all of Barbara Cartland's output and was never disappointed. With tea in hand, Morton approached a table full of possibilities and quickly spotted a hardcover novel in pristine condition. It featured a vibrant color photograph of a scantily clad blonde in a provocative, Marilyn Monroe–ish pose. He was intrigued by its exotic and unpronounceable title: *Nadesjda.*

4

Glennie, who was sleeping on Nat's side of the bed, was awakened by a distant sound of retching. Without stopping to put on her nightgown, she raced to the bathroom, where she found her nude husband on his knees with his head in the toilet bowl. Glennie knew there was nothing she could do for him but asked anyway. With an eerie calm, he waved her away, flushed the toilet, and continued to vomit. Watching her husband's abdomen undulate each time he retched reminded her of the belly dancer she had hired for his thirty-fifth birthday party. That lovely night, inspired by the sensuous writhing of this womanly Turkish delight, she and Nat had indulged in a creative series of mutual pleasurings — not unlike the series they had been involved in less than an hour ago.

"Honey," he had awakened her to ask, "are you at all interested that your beloved husband has a life-threatening erection in his pants?"

"Very interested. Here, let me see it." She had yawned, groping for his fly. "I wouldn't want your death on my hands."

After a cursory examination of his member, Glennie had good-naturedly agreed that he was "indeed in mortal danger," and proceeded to do a good deal more than was necessary to save his life, for which Nat expressed his undying gratitude — before, during, and after the act. She had been surprised at the torrent of flowery and graphically explicit language that was pouring out of him. She had told him that she appreciated the compliments and tried to make him understand that what she had done was "definitely a labor of love" and that she should be thanking him. Nonetheless, he continued to thank her profusely while commandeering her side of the bed and settling into a fetal position. In seconds, while mumbling "Thanks again, sweetie," he had nodded off and slept soundly until he was awakened by a series of unsettling nightmares. Nat had gone from sleeping like an innocent baby to throwing up like a drunken adult.

"I don't know what brought it on," Nat said, lifting his head out of the bowl.

"I hope it wasn't our lovely midnight tryst," she offered worriedly.

"No way," he said, checking his face in the mirror. "More likely it was the sandwich — that cheese may have been spoiled."

"All cheese is spoiled, schmucko," he whined. "Spoiled milk — that's what cheese is made from!"

"Nat, darling," Glennie asked, "who are you talking to?"

"What do you mean *who?*" he asked, taking the robe Glennie offered. "I was talking to you — wasn't I?"

"No, sweetie, you were talking to yourself."

"How do you know?"

"You said 'schmucko' and you never call me 'schmucko' — at least not to my face."

Nat shook his head, slipped into his robe, and punished himself by tying the sash too tightly. Shaken and confused, he turned on the tap and sucked up a mouthful of cold water from the faucet. He gargled loudly, rinsed vigorously, and spit angrily. Glennie stood in the doorway watching in fascination as her husband repeated the gargling, rinsing, and spitting process many more times than she felt was necessary. Concerned for his mental health, she again inquired gently if there was something she might do for him. He shook his head and slurped up another mouthful of water. Had not Glennie turned off the tap, there was no telling how long he would have continued. Glennie spent the rest of what remained of the night catering to his needs, offering him a hot towel, hot tea, and her warmed side of the bed. He warned her not to take it personally if he remained incommunicado for the rest of the night. He vowed that his next conversation would be with Dr. Frucht. He lay awake recalling the details of his disturbing nightmares — and wondering about Dr. Frucht's abilities to interpret them. At dawn he fell asleep mumbling, "That Freudian fuckhead better be good — that — fuckhead — better — be —"

That morning, after learning that Dr. Frucht was willing to rearrange his schedule to make an hour available for him, an energized Nat hopped out of bed, headed for a thirty-second shower, and informed himself, "Nattie, you've got fifty-five minutes to wash, dress, and drive to the Valley — move it!"

Glennie wandered into the bathroom and picked up the damp towel he had used, ineffectually, to dry his body. She watched quietly as he struggled to pull boxer shorts over his damp buttocks and tried to sound casual as she offered to drive him to his appointment.

"No!" he shouted, stripping off the damp shorts he had put on inside out and backward. "I am perfectly capable of driving myself to Tarzana."

She reminded him how sleepless his night had been and how his body must ache from "all that Olympian retching."

"I'm all right. I got some rest."

"Yes, on the rim of the toilet bowl. Nat, if you won't let me drive, let me keep you company, or at least let me call a cab!"

"No!" he said, jamming his sockless feet into his black loafers. "I don't want company!" He snatched a handful of clothes and dashed from the room.

Glennie followed him to the landing and observed his graceless attempt to tuck his shirt into his pants. She shook her head as he barreled down the stairs, past the foyer table, and out the front door. After waiting a moment for him to discover that he had forgotten his keys, Glennie retrieved them from the table and went to the front door, just as he darted from his office carrying a manila folder. He loped to the car, threw the folder in, and settled himself behind the wheel.

"Shit!" Nat said. "I forgot the damn keys! Go get 'em!"

"Why me?" he whined.

"Because I'm belted in!"

"Well, so am I."

It was only after Nat heard himself answer petulantly, "Do I have to do everything myself?" that he was convinced of how deeply in trouble he was.

"Oh, boy, oh, boy," he moaned as he unbelted himself.

"Glennie, toss me my keys, will ya?" he shouted as he ran toward the house.

Had Glennie been privy to her husband's last conversation, she might not have tossed him the keys.

For most of the forty-minute drive to Tarzana, Nat succeeded in shutting down both his brain and his mouth but lost control when he had to cut in front of a truck.

"Hey, hey, dammit!" Nat exploded. "Are you trying to kill us?"

"I am trying not to pass our exit," he snarled, turning sharply toward the off-ramp. "If I were trying to kill us, schmucko, would I be speeding to a shrink's office?"

"Who knows what the hell you would do!"

"If you don't shut your mouth, I'll —"

"You'll what?"

"Shut up! Let's just both of us shut the fuck up!"

The sheer volume of the directive frightened Nat.

"I'm a psycho," he muttered, "a frigging psycho."

"And whose fault is that?" he shot back.

Deciding that it would not be in his best interest to continue the argument, he declined to answer.

Oh, great, Nat thought, seeing an out-of-order sign posted on one of the elevator doors. *I've already lost four minutes of my session with Dr. Frucht.* For a split second he wondered if both elevators were out of order or just the one that had the sign on it.

"What a fucking ambiguous sign," he said, dashing to the stairway. He took two steps at a time and, on the first-floor landing, literally ran into Dr. Trampleasure, who was making her way up the stairs. He knocked a large storage box out of her arms.

"My fault, my fault! I was in such a damn hurry, I didn't look where I was going," he said contritely, stuffing papers back into the box. "I hope these weren't in alphabetical order," he joked.

"They weren't," she said, smiling warmly.

Nat sighed. "Oh, good."

"They were in chronological order. But not to worry," she added quickly, reading the guilt on his face, "in half a wink, my assistant will have every page back where it belongs."

Nat started down the stairs to retrieve some wayward papers when he heard the soft English-accented voice calmly suggest he leave everything where it was and continue on.

"You seemed to be in a particular hurry," the doctor offered.

"Well," he admitted as he ran back up and handed her the box, "I am late for my appointment."

"I assumed you were. You know," she said, "we have met before!"

"Yes, in the lobby, yesterday," he said, continuing up the stairs. "We discussed not using your name in my new novel. Trampleasure, isn't it?"

"Yes," she called up to him, "but what I meant was, didn't we meet somewhere besides the lobby?"

"Yes, in the elevator," Nat called down, stopping at the third-floor landing. "We chatted."

"I was thinking London. Did you ever live in Chelsea?" she asked hopefully.

"No, but I did stay at the Dorchester for nine days last year," he shouted, hesitating at the exit door.

"Drat, I do know you from somewhere — but no matter, please go about your business. I am sure it will come to me!"

It was not her apparent loveliness and her choice of perfume that intrigued Nat, but how earnestly she was pursuing the idea that she knew him.

"Will you be in your office in an hour? I'd like to drop by and see if that thing you're sure will come to you, comes to you."

"Just knock on my door, Mr. Noland."

Pleased that Dr. Trampleasure had given him permission to stop by, Nat exited the stairwell, then popped his head back in.

"Say," he said, speaking rapidly, "I did a television program a couple of years ago — a literary round-table discussion — I was plugging my new novel — *Nadesjda.* Might you have seen the program — it was on C-SPAN?"

When she shook her head and mouthed "Noooooo," Nat smiled, said, "See ya," and bolted.

Nat was aware when he passed the men's room in the hall that he would never get through the session if he did not relieve himself now, so he made a quick U-turn, reached for the doorknob, and prayed that this was one of the rare office buildings where the restrooms did not require a key. It was not! He was about to curse when a man carrying a key attached to a giant toothbrush came out, allowing the keyless Nat to go in and use the urinal. While washing his hands, Nat checked his watch and found that he had lost only two minutes more of his precious forty-five-minute session. He trotted to Dr. Frucht's office, started to open the door, but stopped to check his fly and was glad that he had.

"Just what I need, coming in with my fly open," he said, zipping up. "One more weird thing for the doc to add to my dossier."

"Whoa!" Nat yelped, and jumped back when the door opened just as he reached for the knob.

"Oh, I'm sorry," Dr. Frucht said. "I thought my door may have been locked. I heard a jiggle —"

"Oh, that was me," Nat explained, embarrassed. "I was just, uh —"

"Trying not to add to your dossier?" Dr. Frucht offered.

"Oh, you heard that — I guess I was thinking aloud. Well, good, that's the reason I'm here — I'm sorry I'm late, Doctor, but I had a very bad — oh, yes, I told you on the phone."

"Yes, you did, Mr. Noland," Dr. Frucht said, ushering Nat into the office and offering him some water. Nat was pleasantly surprised to learn that this man whom he had referred to as a "Freudian fuckhead" had just handed him a ten-ounce tumbler of water. On the basis of the tumbler, Nat felt a ray of hope.

He thought, *The man said he'd ordered ten-ounce tumblers and, by God, here they are! A doctor with integrity. I'll have no problem pouring out my guts to this guy!*

Meanwhile, across the hall . . .

After entering her office and setting the storage box atop an open filing cabinet, Dr. Trampleasure lowered herself slowly into a high-backed desk chair and cocked her head in thought. Her head had been cocked figuratively ever since the eccentric American author had bumped into her on the stairwell. She was determined to figure out why she thought they had met previously and hoped to solve the mystery today. She stared idly at the open filing cabinet, wondering if Nat Noland was serious about stopping by after his session.

5

While Nat described his night of romance, retching, and restlessness, and his debilitating struggle to fight the urge to talk to himself, Dr. Frucht sat motionless at his desk, his eyes half shut and the tips of his index fingers resting on his lips. Feeling that he did not have the doctor's full attention, Nat stopped talking.

"Dr. Frucht," he challenged, fingering the manila folder that lay in his lap, "am I boring you?"

"And why do you think that," the doctor said, opening his eyes, "Mr. Noland?"

"You seem distracted."

"I am. By the way, you are fiddling with that folder on your lap. Is it something you wish to talk about?"

"No, actually, it's something I'd like you to read," Nat said, thrusting the folder toward him. "It's a few pages of my new novel. I'd be interested in hearing your opinion — I don't want a critique, but — after you read it, I'll tell you why I thought you should read it. But I had these nightmares last night — should I tell you my nightmares first — I would prefer you read this first — is that okay?"

"There is no okay or not okay. What is offered is what we use," the doctor said, taking the folder, "and you offer pages, so I will read them."

"I named one of the characters in the book Neparia," Nat offered ingenuously. "I saw that name in the lobby directory — I thought it might be of interest — I know it's silly —"

"Nothing is silly," the doctor said, putting on his glasses. "Everything is of interest."

While the doctor read the pages, Nat attempted to read the doctor. At one point he thought he saw the doctor smile but decided that it was more of a sneer. Nat was disturbed by how quickly the man read the ten pages.

Nat thought, *A guy with a German accent can't possibly read English that fast and understand what the hell he's reading — I can't wait to hear what Herr Doktor Speed-Reader comes up with. The ball is in his court.*

"So, Mr. Noland," the doctor asked, neatly slipping the pages back into the folder. "Why did you want me to read this?"

"I thought you might find it instructive."

"And what," the doctor asked, tossing the ball back, "do you think that I might find instructive?"

Damn, Nat thought, *the man just read about a guy who refuses to mate with his mother. What kind of psychiatrist asks why my writing about incest would be instructive?*

"I just thought," Nat offered civilly, "that it might give you a clue as to what makes me tick so erratically, and maybe help us get to the bottom of me."

"Yes, Mr. Noland, it may help us to get, as you say, to the bottom of you," the doctor said, handing Nat the folder, "and I thank you for letting me read it."

That's it? Nat thought. *Just a thank-you for letting me read it? No comment? No opinion?*

Nat was always hesitant to ask anyone to comment on his writing, especially after a friend once asked, "Do you want an *honest* opinion, or would you rather keep our friendship intact?"

Nat thought, *An honest opinion is what I need and what I'm paying this guy for.*

"So, Doctor, what did you think of it?" Nat asked bluntly.

"I think that for our purposes, it would not be helpful for me to critique your work."

"So you didn't like it!"

"That is not what I —"

"It's the subject, right? You think it's blasphemous, don't you? Well, it is," Nat barreled on. "I *meant* it to be! The subject offends you, doesn't it?"

"No, Mr. Noland, I —"

"What then? The writing? The style? Too much dialogue? If you were put off by the lack of descriptive passages, I can understand that. I personally don't like novels that read like stage plays, but in this case, that's what I was going for —"

"Mr. Noland, if you will allow me —"

"Of course. I'm sorry, Doctor. What were you going to say?"

"I wanted to ask how you came to choose the subject for the book."

"I didn't. It chose me, like most of my novels do."

"I see," Dr. Frucht said knowingly. "And do you know at this time how the story will end?"

"I never know — that's what excites me — but I don't think Cain is going to slay Abel."

"You will not follow the Bible's version?"

"No, that's another writer's story, and frankly I can't understand why people buy it. If anybody kills anybody in my book, it won't be Cain slaying Abel. More likely it'll be Abel slaying Cain or maybe Adam slaying Cain — or nobody killing anybody — maybe Eve leaves Adam. You know something, Doctor," Nat said thoughtfully, "I think I started writing this, uh, whatever it turns out to be, because I have been upset by this Garden of Eden myth since I first heard it in Sunday school. I remember crying hysterically and the minister telling me to stop because I was upsetting the other children — and if I didn't stop crying, he couldn't go on with the story. I told him that I didn't want him to go on, which made him angry, and he phoned my mother to come fetch me. I remember sitting next to her in the front seat of the car and crying uncontrollably. She tried to console me, but I was inconsolable. I cried all the way home and didn't even stop when my mom promised to let me help her make marshmallow and Rice Krispies squares."

A tear dropped from Nat's eye as he reached for the ubiquitous box of tissues.

"Do you know what made you cry?" the doctor asked, sliding the box an inch closer to his patient.

"Absolutely," Nat said, snatching a tissue. "When the minister read about Cain slaying Abel, I could not believe it."

"What could you not believe?"

"That a brother would kill a brother," Nat said angrily, dabbing at his eyes. "I don't know why it hit me so hard. Could it be that it's because I was an only child and always wanted a brother — someone to play with? That's too simplistic, isn't it?"

"Maybe, maybe not."

"Hold it!" Nat slapped his forehead. "I just remembered a dream I had two nights ago. It's one I've had a few times — it's definitely in the recurring-dream category — like the other one where I'm flying around my high school gym."

"Can you tell me about the dream?" the doctor asked, leaning back in his flimsy chair.

"Well, I'm lying in a big crib —" Nat started, then paused when he heard the sound of wood splintering. "Uh, Doctor, I think —"

Just as Nat shouted "Your chair is coming apart," the doctor's chair came apart. A nanosecond before it collapsed, Dr. Frucht dextrously ejected himself from it and, without missing a beat, mumbled that he had ordered a sturdier one.

"You were telling me, Mr. Noland," the doctor said, casually kicking the splintered chair into a corner and replacing it with its equally flimsy mate, "before my chair broke, about your recurring dream."

"It's a pretty happy dream," Nat said, impressed by the doctor's composure. "I'm flying around near the ceiling — and the spectators are tossing basketballs at me and I just swat 'em right back — it feels great — and —" Nat stopped. "I'm describing the wrong dream — aren't I?"

"I do not know. Why do you think you told, as you say, the wrong dream?"

"I guess I made a stupid mistake —"

"A mistake?"

"You mean I chose to tell the happy dream?"

"Is the other dream not a happy one?" the doctor asked.

"Well, it's a strange one, and whenever I have it, I wake up feeling depressed," Nat said quietly, then paused.

"Yes, go on, Mr. Noland."

"Well, I'm lying in this giant crib," Nat said after taking a sip of water, "and a big bird flies into the room and hovers over me. The bird is the size of a stork and is wearing a mask and a white cap. It flutters its wings and then reaches down, picks me up in its arms, and takes off. I know birds don't have arms, but this one did. The strangest part is that I watch myself flying out the window while I'm in the crib and crying hysterically. It's like there are two of me."

"The you that was carried out the window," the doctor asked, "what did he look like?"

"Well, for one thing, he wasn't crying, and he was kind of droopy, like he was asleep — or dead. Say, Doctor," Nat offered excitedly, "is it possible that I'm remembering something that really happened?"

"It is possible."

"I don't remember even feeling bad. Do you think that's why I didn't feel sad that the stork took the other me away?" Nat jumped up. "Holy shit, I'm trying to get rid of the other me, aren't I? The me that keeps talking to me! This is fucking fantastic!" Nat picked up the desk clock. "How much time do I have left?"

"Enough time, Mr. Noland," the doctor advised, taking the clock from him, "to say what is, as you put it, er, fucking fantastic."

"Hey, that's exactly how I put it! Good for you, Doc, and it fits! It all fits, doesn't it?"

"And what is that, Mr. Noland?"

"What is what?"

"What is it that fits?"

"The key to my nutsiness," Nat shouted. "That's what fits! Don't you see it?"

"Tell me what *you* see," Dr. Frucht said, "as the key to your nutsiness."

In Nat's book, his psychiatrist's stock went soaring when he repeated the words "fucking" and "nutsiness" with no hint of sarcasm in his voice.

"I see what you're doing, Doctor," Nat said. "You think it'll mean more to me if *I* put the pieces together. Am I right?"

"There is no right or wrong," the doctor offered.

"Okay," Nat agreed, checking the clock. "I hope you don't cut me off when that red light goes on."

"Contrary to what you have heard," Dr. Frucht said, "we do allow patients to finish a thought, especially" — he smiled — "if the thought may be the key to his 'nutsiness.' "

"Okay, my nutsiness — here goes!" Nat said, pacing rapidly back and forth. "That recurring dream, with me lying in a giant crib and the stork taking away the baby that I think is me? Well, I think I've had other dreams where I've felt that same thing," Nat answered, straining to remember.

"Could you recall one?"

"Well, there's this one," Nat said, rubbing his brow, "but I haven't dreamed it for a long, long time. I'm in this crib —"

"The giant crib?"

"No, a regular-size crib. I'm lying there, and someone picks me up and then puts me down — two or three times — and the last time I'm picked up, I don't get put down — but I'm still in the crib and I start bawling and the more I bawl, the bigger the crib gets. Hey, there's that giant crib again. Well, that's it," Nat said, sitting down on the wicker couch. "Gave you a lot of garbage to work with, didn't I?"

"What garbage are you referring to, Mr. Noland?"

"You know, in that other dream — with the big white bird wearing a white mask and cap, who picked me up — could it have been a doctor or a nurse — or my parents?"

"Ah, yes, Mr. Noland," Dr. Frucht said meaningfully, "do you know who were your birth parents?"

"Not really," Nat said, having expected the question. "They died the day I was born. My adoptive parents were rather protective. They never gave me too many of the details. My dad told me that my natural father died in an auto accident while driving my mother to the hospital, and she died a few hours later after giving birth to me — pretty dramatic beginning, eh, Doc?"

"Yes, dramatic," Dr. Frucht agreed, ignoring the blinking red light. "And were you not curious, Mr. Noland, to find out more about your birth parents?"

"For a lot of years I wasn't, but lately I've been thinking —" Nat hesitated when he saw the blinking light.

"Yes, Mr. Noland, you were thinking — ?"

"That I'd like to —" Nat stopped short. "Your red light is blinking, Doctor."

"So it is," the doctor said, clicking it off.

"Are you going to send me packing?"

"You do not have to pack, Mr. Noland. Please to continue."

"Well, I was thinking of hiring a private detective to search for any aunts, uncles, or cousins who may be out there. Maybe," he said with a laugh, "I've got a crazy uncle who talks to himself. Can this thing I do be genetic? Is that possible?"

"Anything is possible," the doctor answered, and stood up, signaling the end of the session. "But it would surprise me if such a gene exists."

"Are you saying that I shouldn't hire a private eye?"

"Mr. Noland, all information is helpful, whether the sources come from the world outside or from the world inside your head."

6

Nat had every intention of going straight home but hesitated on his way to the elevator when the doctor's words "all information is helpful" flashed through his head. He looked back at Dr. Frucht's office and then across the corridor to Dr. Trampleasure's. He remembered her saying they had met before, and was confident that she would remember where and when. Nat was not one who believed in fated events, but he did enjoy when a coincidence occurred that appeared to be the work of outside forces. He paused at Dr. Trampleasure's door and reflected on why he was nervous about knocking. There was no question that she was attractive, and if he weren't happily married, she would be high on his list of women whom he would ask to dinner. He considered leaving when he reminded himself that she was a doctor, a Ph.D.

"Yeah, but a Ph.D. in what?" Nat mumbled softly.

"Hey, I heard that!" Nat said, smiling. "I

was talking to myself and I knew I was! How about that! My sessions with Frucht are bearing fruit!" He cringed at his little joke as he knocked on the doctor's door.

"Ah, Mr. Noland," said a broadly smiling Dr. Trampleasure. "I'm pleased that you decided to visit. I was not sure you would. Do come in," she said, opening the door wide. "I apologize for the disarray."

"Disarray?" He laughed. "I've never seen an office more arrayed."

The office was sparsely but tastefully furnished. Two watercolors caught his eye — one of wildflowers and the other a mountain landscape. He considered the subjects corny but found the works pleasing.

"Yours?" he guessed, noticing the paintings were signed with a tiny *g t.*

"I'm afraid so," she said apologetically.

"They're very good — quite affecting," he added.

"You're too kind. Until I can afford Monet, they'll have to do. Won't you have a seat?" she said, indicating one of the two club chairs in a chintz-draped alcove.

Before Nat had settled in his chair, she announced eagerly, "Mr. Noland, it has come to me — as I knew it would — that we *have* met before!"

"You mean before that day in the lobby?"

"Yes, and had you arrived two minutes earlier, I would *not* have been able to tell you where and under what circumstances."

"Are you saying we know each other?" Nat said, examining her face for a clue.

"Yes — and I daresay," she said excitedly, "we knew each other rather well."

"Rather well? Are you sure?" Nat asked, mirroring her excitement. "I can't believe that I would forget knowing you."

"It was a good many years ago."

"Even so, I'd remember you," he offered gallantly.

"When I recall the circumstances for you," she said, smiling sadly, "you may understand why you might not want to remember."

"The circumstances," Nat asked, grimacing, "were they what you might call embarrassing?"

"One might." She smiled. "But not after all these years. May I ask you a personal question?"

"Of course," he replied, intrigued, "but only if you'll allow me to ask you one."

"No more than fair. I'm expecting that we'll have many, many questions for each other. Ready for the first one?"

"I guess so. I don't know why I'm nervous. I have no major skeletons in my closet. Okay, what's your first question?"

"You were adopted, weren't you?"

Nat was taken aback. He had never expected this question.

"Were you eavesdropping on my session with Dr. Frucht?" he asked suspiciously.

"I assure you I was not." She laughed. "So I take it that you were adopted?"

"Yes, but how in the world would you know that? Does this have anything to do with your being a Ph.D.?"

"Not a thing," she said. "It has to do with my having an excellent memory for faces."

"You've seen my face before, Doctor?"

"Oh, yes!"

"Have I seen yours before?" Nat asked, peering at her face.

"Many times."

"Many times?" Nat strained to remember. "Where would I have seen it?"

"In a moment," she answered, suppressing a smile. "Is Noland the name of your adoptive parents?"

"Yes, it is."

"And Nat is the name they chose for you?"

"Yes — Nathaniel, actually," Nat responded, his curiosity and impatience growing.

"Nathaniel Noland," she repeated sadly.

"Had I known your name, I might have tried contacting you years ago."

"I am confused, Dr. Trampleasure. Why would you have tried to contact me?"

"Look at me closely, Mr. Noland," she suggested, leaning forward in her chair. "Search your memory. Do I not look familiar to you?"

Nat did as he was told. He stared at her beautiful, unlined face and searched her large green eyes for a clue.

"I'm sorry," he said, "but you do not look even vaguely familiar. The only thing I recognize is the lovely scent you're wearing. It's Opium, isn't it?"

She nodded. "Mr. Noland," she asked, turning her profile to him, "do you not remember what you said about my nose?"

"Well, if I didn't say that it's one of the world's prettiest, then I wasn't paying attention. But frankly," he admitted, "I don't remember you or your perfect nose."

"But," she exploded, "you just did! Those are almost the words you used."

"What words?"

" 'You and your perfect nose,' " she answered excitedly. "The day we parted, you said, 'I'll miss seeing you and that perfect nose of yours.' I can tell you now how thrilled I was to hear you pay me that compliment — I remember blushing. I think you did, too. You were a rather shy young man in those days, weren't you?"

"I was a shy young man," he agreed, "but I don't remember being a shy young man in your presence. Now, exactly where was it," Nat asked skeptically, "that you heard me say that about your nose?"

Either she is mistaking me for someone else, he thought, *or I'm a good deal nuttier than I thought I was.*

Nat was sorely tempted to run across the hall to consult with Dr. Frucht.

"Are you sure it was me, Dr. Trampleasure? Could it be that you've mixed me up with someone else?"

"No, I haven't. You were quite a bit younger, and you have added weight, height, and facial hair, but it was you who made me blush."

"And where were we," he asked pointedly, "when I made you blush?"

"I remember precisely. On the back lawn of the Creedmore Preparatory School. It was a dreary day and we were alone. We were talking and holding hands. Surely you remember that!"

"No," he said forcefully. "I do not remember Creedmore Preparatory and I do not remember being on its back lawn and I am positive, Dr. Trampleasure, that I never held your hand. In fact, I had never heard the name Trampleasure until I saw it in the directory!"

"At Creedmore my name wasn't Trampleasure. It was Kent — Gertrude Kent. I used my mother's maiden name."

"Why?"

"My father was in British Intelligence, and he and Mother felt that I would be less in harm's way if I didn't use his name while away at school. All very James Bond–like!" she said conspiratorially. "It didn't make much sense to me, but I rather liked having an alias. You weren't Nathaniel Noland then, were you?"

"Oh? Who was I?"

"Buddy — Buddy Keebler! You were searching out your birth parents — and you must have found them."

"Not yet — Buddy who?" he roared.

"*Keebler!* Oh, come on, Buddy, you must remember that — or," she said, eyeing him warily, "is there some reason you don't care to remember?"

Nat took a deep breath and stared at this attractive English princess who was slowly morphing into a relentless prosecuting attorney.

"May I ask you a question?" he asked forthrightly.

"Certainly," she allowed graciously.

"Who are you and what kind of Ph.D. are you?"

"I am, as I told you, Gertrude Trampleasure, and I have a doctorate in empathology."

"You are a doctor of empathology?"

"Yes, I am a practicing empathologist," she responded, smiling her professional smile. "It's a rather new discipline developed in Wales by Dr. J. J. Fellows Bracebahn."

"Are you practicing empathology on me right now? And just what is an empathologist?"

"Later!" she said, striding to her filing cabinet and retrieving a worn photo album. She opened it to where she had placed a bookmark.

"Who are these two people?" she challenged, thrusting the album into his lap and tapping her finger on a three-by-five photo. "I dare you to tell me that you don't remember them!"

Nat peered at a color photo of a teenage couple — and gasped.

"That's me!" he shouted. "That's me — that's my face! Dammit, it's me, but I don't remember posing for this picture!"

"Well, I certainly do," she offered, pointing to the girl in the photo. "Remember that girl?"

Wow, he thought. *That lovely girl in the pink organdy dress could easily have evolved into this lovely woman who's hovering over my shoulder.*

"Wait," he muttered, examining the picture closely. "This couldn't be me!"

"But a moment ago," she argued, "you said that that was your face."

"That *is* my face," he admitted, looking at it closely, "but *that* is not my shirt and *that* is not my jacket. I have never owned a striped shirt or a jacket that color!"

"Every boy at Creedmore did. It was the dress code."

"But I have never been to Creedmore," he pleaded, "and until you mentioned it, I had never heard of the place."

"Mr. Noland, it has been more than twenty years since we last chatted, but I must tell you," she said, clearly trying to stem an unexpected flow of emotion, "your voice has not changed a whit. The timbre remains quite distinctive. I recall hearing you read a short essay in our English class and complimenting you on how well it was written and what a fine voice you had — 'John Gielgud–ish,' I added." She smiled. "And you asked, 'Who is John Gielgudish?'

When I explained that I was referring to the actor John Gielgud, we both laughed so hard. You must remember that!"

"I'm afraid I don't," Nat answered, noting the disappointment in her face.

"I was so sure you would. You even repeated the John Gielgudish thing to our classmates — and they all roared."

"Dr. Trampleasure, at the risk of seeming arrogant, I have many times received compliments on my speaking voice, and I swear, by whatever gods are still in power, that I do not remember you or the Gielgudish incident or the Creedmore Preparatory School — and as for this," he said, referring to the photo, "I don't know how or why, but, for whatever perverse reason, someone has superimposed my head on this body."

"I can assure you, Mr. Noland, that photo was snapped by Laylah Leadbeller and has never been out of this album since I put it there."

"Well, to put it crudely, it ain't me!"

Nat's insistence dampened Dr. Trampleasure's enthusiasm. She'd been sure that his seeing the photo would jog his memory. She'd decided not to show him another photo in the album when, suddenly, Nat clapped his hands.

"Hey, that girl who snapped the picture — did you say her name was Lalia Leadbelly?"

"*Laylah* Lead*beller.* You do remember redheaded, lavender-eyed Laylah? How could you not!"

Nat was surprised by the sensual note that crept into her voice when she spoke Laylah's name. It was now becoming a game he wanted to continue playing.

"This Laylah Leadbeller," he ventured, "why do you think I should remember her?"

"Oh, come on now! You're teasing me. For almost a year, you and 'Luscious Laylah' were inseparable."

"I'm sorry, Dr. Trampleasure, but unless I'm suffering from selective amnesia, Luscious Laylah is not memorable — at least not to me, but I'll bet she is to Buddy Keebler."

"Oh" — she sighed defeatedly — "I was sure you knew her."

"Well, I don't!"

"Why did your eyes light up when I mentioned her name?"

"Because Laylah Leadbeller is a *great* name," he said, jotting it down.

"Oh? Shall we be seeing Laylah's name in one of your novels, Mr. Noland?"

"It's possible. I don't know if it interests you, but I may retitle my new book with a name I cadged from your lobby directory."

"Not Trampleasure, I trust," she said icily.

"No, you're safe. It's set in biblical times, and Trampleasure just wouldn't work — although *Jertrude* might."

His attempt at levity was lost on her as she lifted the photo out of her album. She stared at Nat for a moment, then at the photo, unsure of how to proceed. Nat half expected her to tear up the snapshot and throw it in his face.

"You may be interested in this," she said, taking another photo from the album and handing it to him, "particularly what's written on the back."

Nat looked at the handwritten words that read *Buddy and Gert — July 1972 A.D.* He wondered how she wanted him to react, but before he could ask, she handed him a third photo.

He looked at it and smiled. The photo featured the same couple, Gertrude and Buddy, in a passionate, lip-locked embrace. He was spooked by how much Buddy Keebler's hair and head shape resembled his at that age. On the back was written *Buddy and Gert A.L.*

"Doctor, may I ask what 'Buddy and Gert A.D.' and 'Buddy and Gert A.L.' signify?"

"The A.D. stands for Anno Domini and the A.L. stands for" — she sighed — "After Laylah."

"I get it," he said proudly, having figured it out. "This is the kiss that separated the inseparable Buddy and Laylah."

"Yes, I was the *hussy* who came between her — and —" She sighed again. "I was so sure that you were the —"

"The *hussar?*" he offered, making her smile. "I wish I were."

Nat took a long last look at the two photos before handing them back. He then looked squarely at the doctor.

That lucky bastard! he thought. "Apparently, by not being Buddy Keebler, I missed out on something really wonderful."

He was shocked to hear the doctor say, "Well, aren't you kind! I am flattered that you think that. Thank you!"

"You're welcome," he said sheepishly, realizing that, once again, unknowingly, he had given voice to his thoughts. "I'm glad you feel that way — uh, flattered," he added.

"Well, it's not surprising that I do — considering how much you and Buddy look alike. You two could be twins!"

"Twins? That's interesting," he mumbled.

"I have often wondered what Buddy grew up to look like, and now I know. I'll wager he looks just like you, which, if he does, is his good fortune."

"Well, now *I* am flattered." He smiled. "Thank you!"

Both were uncomfortable with the blatant flirtation, but neither felt compelled to discontinue.

"I just had an idea," she said, tapping her chin coquettishly. "I have not seen Buddy Keebler since he left Creedmore, and I was thinking that if he grew up to look like you, it might be a lovely idea to try locating him."

"May I help?" Nat offered eagerly. "It could be to both of our advantages. We were both adopted, and it is within the realm of possibility that we are twin brothers, but if it turns out that we aren't, at least you'll have found an old, dear friend who may or may not still look like me, and, he may be — what, unhappily unmarried?"

The moment the words escaped his mouth, Nat felt like biting his tongue, and he did. After letting out a subdued "Owww," he apologized for his unthinking remark. He was about to say "I don't know what made me say that" when he realized that he *did* know. It was his graceless way of informing her that he was happily married and that the harmless little flirtation they were having was

74

just that. Before he could find the proper words, the doctor put him at ease.

"I cannot imagine," she offered, smiling warmly, "that Buddy Keebler would be un-attached, but one never knows, does one?"

"No, and because we don't, I think we ought to track the man down."

" 'We,' Mr. Noland?"

Nat was suddenly energized. "You are not going to believe this, Doctor, but just min-utes ago, I was discussing with Dr. Frucht the possibility of hiring a private detective to search for information about my birth par-ents — and Buddy Keebler might very well have that information. Shall we join forces?"

"Yes, let's." She offered him the photos. "Would you like to have these? I am sure a private detective would find them useful and — I think your wife might find them in-teresting."

"Well, I know she'll find this one," he said, indicating the photo of the lip-locked couple, "*most* interesting." Nat laughed un-comfortably, thanked her for her time and interest, and promised to return the photos on his next visit to Dr. Frucht. At the door, she extended her slender white hand to shake, which, for a split second, he consid-ered kissing. He shook it and muttered, "See ya, Doc!"

★ ★ ★

As Nat made his way to the elevator, he thought of his wife and realized that when he told her about his brief encounter with this attractive empathologist, Glennie was bound to ask what an empathologist was, and all he could tell her was that it was a new discipline developed by a Welsh doctor, J. J. Feller Bracebomb or something. He thought about going back and asking Dr. Trampleasure to explain what empathology was, but he didn't trust himself to spend any more time with someone who looked and smelled as good as she did.

On the drive home, at every red light, Nat studied the photos of Buddy Keebler and Gertrude Trampleasure, and the more intently he analyzed them, the more certain he was that he and Buddy Keebler were twins.

"Hey," Nat giggled as he studied the photo, "maybe, like on the old *Patty Duke Show*, we're identical first cousins!"

"Genetically impossible!" he argued.

"Hey there, twin bro," he said, addressing the photo, "how about if, instead of talking to myself, I talk to you?"

A sense of well-being settled over Nat when he heard no response.

7

London

Morton Quigley never could have imagined that his rainy-day visit to Browse and Steep's bookstore would turn his life upside down. When he arrived home wet, disheveled, and late for the family dinner, he offered his wife an apology and a damp, gift-wrapped present, both of which she declined. Sarah was not happy that her husband was in no condition to greet their dinner guests, who were due to arrive within minutes.

"Morton, you can't bribe me out of the foul mood you've put me in by presenting me with this puny box of chocolates. We've a dozen guests, and most all of them are chocoholics," she scolded, handing back her present. "What were you thinking?"

"I am sorry, luv, but I'm not bribing you with a puny box of chocolates. I'm trying to bribe you with a great new romance novel — hardcover — it has won all kinds of awards," he lied. "It's a special, special book."

"Well, Mr. Special, Special," she groused, tossing it into a drawer, "go change — and quickly!"

The evening started well, with one of Sarah's chocoholic friends presenting her with a giant tin of assorted Swiss chocolates, and it ended well, with Sarah apologizing to Morton for her shrewish behavior and assuring him that, in spite of all of his "failings," she loved him deeply. As they got ready for bed, she thanked him for being such a gracious host. "And most of all," she gushed, hugging the book, "for buying me this special, special novel. Perfect timing, darling, I had nothing to read tonight."

"I hope you like it," he said, stepping out of his trousers. "There was something about that book that caught my eye."

"I wonder what that would be?" she chided, eying the voluptuous blonde on the cover. "The title, perhaps?"

"Definitely the title," he said, kissing her cheek, "and her lovely titties — remind me of yours."

"G'wan, you." She chuckled. "Say, luv, how would you pronounce this honeypot's name? Na-deesha?"

"Not Na-deesha. I'd say Nadesha."

"You think? But what about the *j* and the *d*?" she asked, pointing to the title, *Nadesjda.*

"The *j* and *d* are silent . . . like the *ph* in fart," Morton joked, dashing to the bathroom. "You start reading your Nadesha and I'll draw my bath."

"Nathaniel Noland has done it again! He has written an involving and sensuous love story that contains enough mystery and intrigue to delight the most discriminating reader."
— Jay Quiller Harcourt

"Nadesjda, who inhabits the pages of Nat Noland's most erotic novel since *The Nibbler,* is the woman every man dreams of meeting and every woman dreams of being. Viva Nadesjda!"
— Uli Boonshoft

"I hope Mr. Noland is planning to write *Nadesjda II* and *Nadesjda III.* This fascinating, fulsome fox deserves to be heard from again and again."
— Jay B. Thalinger

Sarah always enjoyed discovering new authors and went to the back cover flap to read his bio. Her eyes popped when she saw Nathaniel Noland's photo.

"Morton! Morton!" she shrieked, bolting into the bathroom, where her husband was soaking in the tub. "You dear, silly boy! How in the world did you do this?"

"Do what?" he asked innocently.

"This!" she said, laughing and pointing to the photo. "You devil, you! How did you replace the author's photo with yours? You said that this was a special, special book — and it is, my darling!"

Morton had no idea what his wife was shrieking about, and he asked for his reading glasses.

"Your reading glasses?" She laughed, handing them to him. "Darling, did you forget what you look like?"

"Oh, m-my God," he stuttered, staring at the photo, "th-this could be me!"

"Could be? Oh, come off it, Morty, it *is* you!"

"It's not," he said, peering at the photo. "This is not me!"

"It's perfect," she insisted. "Did you do this on your computer?"

"Sarah, I didn't do it! This man is Nathaniel Noland," he said, tapping the photo. "Look here, he's holding a pipe! Sarah, did you ever see me smoking a pipe?"

"No, but I've seen you smiling that smile." She laughed again, touching his mouth: "Those are *your* teeth, darling, are they not?"

"No, they are *his* teeth," he said, peering at the photo, "but they do resemble mine, don't they?"

Sensing her husband's discomfort, Sarah calmly took the book from him. "Morton," she said, examining the color photo, "this is uncanny. He has your hairline, your color eyes, your lips — he could be your twin brother."

Morton Quigley took the book back and carefully studied the author's lips, eyes, and hairline.

"Morton, you don't have a twin brother, do you?"

"Obviously I do, and he's an American novelist named Nathaniel Noland."

8

Carefree, Arizona

Jed Noland was elated to hear his son's voice on the phone, asking if it was "all right to pop in."

"Well, I don't know," Jed joked, then called out, "Bertha, it's Natey — he and Glennie want to pop in. Should we let them?"

"Just a 'pop in'? Hmm," Bertha mused, smiling. "Where are they?"

"In a cab, coming from the Scottsdale airport."

"In that case, they can come."

Nat and Glennie were welcomed with broad smiles, warm embraces, loving kisses, and an offer from Bertha Noland to whip up a batch of her homemade Belgian waffles.

"Do you know, Glennie," Bertha said, "young Natey once ate four of my —"

"Ma, before you start reminiscing, take a look at these — and look at them carefully." Nat handed her two photos.

"Ahhh, how sweet, Natey! Where did you

find these?" Bertha handed them to her husband. "I've never seen these before. Have you, Jed?"

"Say, who's the little fox you're smoochin' with, son?" Nat's father chided. "You never told me about her. She's a looker" — he laughed, putting his arm around his daughter-in-law — "but your Glennie's got her beat ten ways."

"You were sooo handsome, Natey, and you look so dapper in that jacket. I must be getting old — I don't remember that jacket. Is that the one you hated, the one Aunt Harriet gave you for Christmas?"

"No, Mums, I hated that purple sweater she knitted for me. Take another look. You sure this is me?"

"Of course it's you. Who else would it be?"

"How about you, Dad? Do you think that's me in those photos?"

"Well, son," he said thoughtfully, looking up from the photos, "I think that you wouldn't be flying here if there wasn't something about these snapshots that's buggin' ya. I think you want me to say that *is* you in the photo, so you can say that it *isn't* you. Am I right?"

"Boy, Dad, you are smart! Folks," Nat announced, "that is *not* me!"

"And you never met that girl, right, son?"

"Actually, Dad, I did meet her, but only a couple of days ago. She's the one who gave me these pictures. Now, Dad, Mums," Nat said, taking his mother's hand, "it would seem that, out there somewhere, I have a twin brother, and I need you to tell me everything you know about my adoption and my birth parents. You've told me that my father died in a car crash on the way to the hospital and that my mother died in childbirth. Do you know the name of the hospital — or the city?"

"We were told it was in Boston, Massachusetts," his mother said, "but that's all."

"It's not clear, but I think you were cared for by a foster mother for a couple of months," his father added. "I think they said that she brought you to the adoption agency. We never got to meet her."

"You were the cutest thing, just nine weeks old and so bright and active," his mother boasted. "You know, when you were seven months old, you stood up and took your first steps."

"You did," his father concurred. "We told you that, didn't we?"

"Many, *many* times — and that I was running before I was seven and a half months."

"Nobody ever believes us when we tell them," his mother added.

"Mums, I don't know if I do."

"Nat," Jed insisted, "our pediatrician, Dr. Baimler, said that he had never seen a more coordinated infant."

"You did everything early," his mother said. "You teethed early, and you were talking before you were a year — and by thirteen months —"

"— I was saying whole sentences, and at a year and a half," Nat added mockingly, "I recited the Lord's Prayer while riding my tricycle."

"It's true, Natey," his mother insisted. "And we have those eight-millimeter home movies to prove all of it. You've seen them."

"Yes, I have. So, to sum up, I was nine weeks old when you adopted me, and by all standards, I was a mental and physical phenom."

"You were a pistol," Jed agreed. "All of our friends were amazed."

"And jealous," Bertha added.

"Did it ever occur to anyone that my birth records might have been tampered with?"

"Yes, Sheila and Ron, our next-door neighbors, suggested that." Jed laughed. "They even doubted it when I showed them your birth certificate."

"Ron accused *us* of doctoring it," his mother chimed in. "I tell you, Natey, you were a much admired baby."

"You know," Nat said thoughtfully, "to enhance a baseball player's value, agents have been known to list their players as being a couple of years younger than their actual age."

"Yeah," Nat agreed with himself. "That same ethic might apply to the owner of an adoption agency. Sure," he continued, gathering steam, "most couples would pay a premium to adopt the youngest infant possible. The younger the baby, the higher the fee. It's just good business!"

"Nat, darling," Glennie asked softly, "were you talking to us or were you thinking out loud?"

"Huh? I guess both. I was thinking about the adoption process and, in particular, my adoption."

Being loving parents, Jed and Bertha Noland were troubled to see their son so agitated, and they struck a deal with him. If he calmed down and had some of his mother's made-from-scratch Belgian waffles, she would search out everything she had that was relevant to his adoption.

While Nat ate, his mother rummaged through boxes of memorabilia. She dug up a color photo of him when he was Buddy Keebler's age. Nat compared it to the Keebler photo and shook his head in amazement. "There is no doubt! These two guys are identical twins!"

"Identical, hmmm," his father said pensively. "Oh, my goodness! Natey, I just remembered something your mother said the first time we saw you. Do you remember what you said, Bertha?"

"I do. I said, 'Jed, this is *the* most beautiful baby I have ever laid eyes on,' because you were *that* beautiful," she said, turning to Nat.

"And do you remember what *I* said, Bertha?"

"No, Jed, I don't. All I remember is staring at the baby. What *did* you say?"

"I said, 'Wrap him up, we'll take him — *and as many like him as you've got.*' "

"Oh, yes." Bertha laughed. "I do remember."

"And do you remember the Grimshades' reaction to my little joke — and the odd look that passed between them?"

"No, Jed, I was too busy counting sweet little fingers and toes."

"The Grimshades?" Nat asked. "Who were they?"

"The couple who ran the agency," Jed explained.

"How do you spell Grimshade?"

"You still collecting weird names, son? I'm not sure how they spelled it, but I think Mums still has their letters."

"I sure do," she said, rummaging through the carton. "I knew that one day you'd want all this information."

"Dad, tell me about the Grimshades — and the look they exchanged."

"Well, when I said I'd take as many like you as they had, they froze and then looked at each other. It was kind of a two-part look. Mrs. Grimshade repeated my line and started to laugh — he did, too, but his was nervous. If they hadn't laughed that weird way, I might not have remembered it."

"Dad, I'll bet they had twin boys available and opted to split them up."

"You may be right, son. Split them up and get twice the money."

"Natey, dear," Nat's mother said, handing him a letter, "I hope this will be of some help."

" 'Gelliard Grimshade Adoption Services,' " Nat read, " 'Boston, Mass.' "

"Yes, you're a Boston baby, dear. I doubt this agency still exists —"

"I'll be surprised if it does," his father offered. "It's been a lot of years since —"

"Why don't we find out," Nat said, striding to the phone.

Nat dialed the agency's number and was informed that it was not a working number.

"How stupid. I forgot the area code," he said, tapping in Boston's area code. He was surprised and delighted to hear a pleasant voice answer.

"Gelliard Grimshade Adoption Services. Can you hold?"

Nat held, but after suffering through a full chorus and a half of a cutesy recording of "You Must Have Been a Beautiful Baby," he hung up and redialed.

"Look, this is too important for any more holding," he barked. "I would like to speak to Mr. or Mrs. Grimshade, now!"

"It will have to be Mrs. Grimshade. Mr. Grimshade is not with us anymore. May I ask the nature of your call?"

"An adoption!"

"An adoption. What did you say your name is?"

"I didn't, but it's Nathaniel Noland."

"*The* Nathaniel Noland?" she squealed. "The author?"

When Nat confirmed that he was *the* Nathaniel Noland, she turned civil.

"Oh, Mr. Noland, may I tell you what a big fan I am," she trilled. "And so is Mrs.

Grimshade. She'll be so thrilled to speak with you. I'll put you through."

Nat had to endure only a few more bars of their theme song before being greeted enthusiastically.

"Well, well, Mr. Nathaniel Noland," Mrs. Grimshade gushed, "I'm thrilled to be speaking with you. I've read all of your books. Now, what can we do for you?"

"Well, it's about my adoption —"

"Oh? Have you made inquiries with us about placing an infant with you?"

"No, I was referring to my own adoption. Your agency placed me with my folks."

"Oh, did we?" Mrs. Grimshade asked, flustered. "We've had so many clients —"

"Well, can you look it up someplace, and find out if I've got a twin brother?"

"You wish to know if you have a twin brother?" she asked hesitantly. "Uh, can you hold for a brief moment, Mr. Noland?"

During the "brief moment" of holding, a slow-boiling Nat listened to three full choruses of "Beautiful Baby." The fourth was interrupted by the voice of a deadly earnest Mrs. Grimshade. "Mr. Noland, I would like to answer your question, but I am not able to — that is, not on the phone. However, if you can come to our office, we may be able to help you. My husband insists that he be present."

"Your husband," Nat said, shaking his head. "I was told that he's, uh —"

"— not with us anymore?" she said, obviously annoyed. "Oh dear, I have instructed Ivy — she's new here — not to put it that way. It is true that my husband is no longer with us in the *agency,* but he is still with *me,* what's left of him. He's lost so much weight since his stroke — poor Gelliard has very little appetite. Nothing appeals to him — eats nothing but Cheerios and —"

"Mrs. Grimshade," Nat pleaded, his temper rising, "why can't you tell me whether or not I have a twin brother?"

"I understand your impatience, Mr. Noland, but it is rather complicated. If it is important to you, I'm afraid you will have to make a trip to Boston."

It took Glennie just one phone call to secure Nat a flight to Boston, and hers to Los Angeles. At the airport, during the round of hugs and kisses, Nat assured his parents that he would call when or if the Grimshade Agency had shed any light on his heritage.

An hour, an hour, what am I going to do in this damn lounge for an hour? was the mantra that had been running through Nat's brain since he heard that his flight to Boston had been delayed.

"What do all serious novelists do with time on their hands?"

"Write!"

"Right, we write, and we'll do it right in this damn lounge! Where's my laptop?"

There were one or two sensitive souls "in this damn lounge" who tried not to stare at a fellow passenger who was having a spirited conversation with himself about the setting for the next chapter of his book. The last exchange the eavesdroppers heard was:

"Let's get out of the friggin' Garden of Eden!"

"Where outside — and what do we call it?"

"I don't care — just start typing!"

OUTSIDE THE GARDEN OF EDEN

"My sister will not lie with thee until she finds thee Twice Worthy."

The words "Twice Worthy" were seared in Cain's brain and he repeated them as he ran through an unfamiliar forest, searching for the dark woman, the only woman on earth with the power to make erect his penis. Cain knew not in which direction Neparia had fled, but he knew that if he did but follow his heart, he would find her — and thus prove to Dada that there exists one who is named Neparia and one who did not spring from his ribs or Eve's loins!

After a fruitless day of searching in a great green grove, Cain fell to his knees and wept as he cried out for Neparia — and did continue to weep and cry out her name until sleep overtook him.

As dawn broke, Cain awoke with a premonition that on this day he would see Neparia and she, on seeing Cain, would find him Twice Worthy! As Cain breathed the morning air, he became aware of an enchanting aroma. He looked about and did find its source — it was lying beside him. The heavenly scent was emanating from a luscious red apple — the same cursed fruit the Serpent enticed Eve to convince Adam to eat. Cain looked about for the Serpent and saw, peering out at him from behind a tree, not an evil, slithering snake but the beautiful, lithesome Neparia, holding an apple. She did bite into her apple and, with a nod of her head, bade Cain to eat of his fruit. Cain, invited to taste of life, bit deeply into the apple and then did take a cautious step toward Neparia, who strode toward him. Cain had never before seen a human walk in the manner Neparia did — her full hips swaying gracefully from side to side, her soft, fleshy breasts moving up and down in slow, rhythmic arcs. He had no sense of Neparia's feelings for him, but from the erectness of his penis, Neparia could see how sincere were his feelings for her.

With his mouth full of apple, Cain did touch his lips to Neparia's and together they kissed and chewed each other's forbidden fruit — their hands caressing each other's body, searching for the heretofore unexplored areas for pleasure and pleasuring.

And in the days and nights that did follow, they continued their search for new and exciting carnal knowledge — oft succeeding. They spoke of their adventure as a "labor of love."

Later, as they sat by the stream, a happy but curious Cain did ask Neparia, "What is it that I have done, that has made me, in thine eyes, Twice Worthy?"

Neparia kissed his brow and did recite a rhyme,

'Tis Once Worthy that thou didst weep
    whilst calling my name.
And Twice Worthy that thy tears were
    shed without shame.

9

Boston, Mass.

It was clear that the adoption agency had done well for the Gelliard Grimshades. Nat was warmly welcomed into their large, stately home by an elderly housekeeper who informed him that they would "be down shortly." Nat followed the sensibly shod woman down an expensively carpeted hall and into a musty, well-appointed sitting room. When asked if there was anything she might get for him, Nat thought, *Yeah, the goddamned unabridged story of my conception and adoption,* but instead he asked for a glass of water.

Nat lowered himself into a club chair and wondered what in heaven's name he was doing here in Boston. *Why did Grimshade insist I fly here? Why couldn't he tell me on the phone whether or not I have a twin brother?*

As he had this thought, Nat was aware that he was actually thinking it and not giving voice to it. *Hey, two visits to Doc*

Frucht and I'm cured!

Nat had a broad grin on his face when he turned to acknowledge a smiling, blond-haired Sally Grimshade, who deftly maneuvered her ninety-one-year-old, wheelchair-bound spouse into the room.

She's a century younger than the old fart, he thought, *must be at least the third Mrs. Grimshade.*

"My husband is so pleased you've come," Mrs. Grimshade offered, gently patting down her husband's unkempt hair. "I am not sure why, but he insists you hear the circumstances of your birth and adoption from him."

Dr. Grimshade managed a droopy-lipped sneer and lisped, "Yesh, the shircumshtances — from me."

"That nasty old stroke has taken a terrible toll on dear Gelliard," Mrs. Grimshade explained as she jockeyed his wheelchair directly to where Nat was seated. Nat tried not to grimace as he looked into the twisted, ashen face of the deadest-looking live person he had ever seen.

"He's hard of hearing," Mrs. Grimshade explained brightly, "but he's an excellent lip reader. His speech may be impaired, but his memory is keen. Last night" — she giggled — "he said to me, 'Sally, do you remember

96

that ivory and gold pendant I gave you on our — ' "

Sally Grimshade stopped abruptly when Gelliard tapped the tip of his cane to her chin.

"Shit — Shally!" he barked. "Shit down — and be quiet!"

Dutifully, Sally sat as Gelliard tilted his head back and peered at Nat through the reading part of his thick bifocals. He stared for a long time before his palsied hand reached out and brushed Nat's cheek. Nat wondered if the old man's rheumy eyes were naturally watery or if they teared up on seeing someone he had once placed in a good home.

"Mishter Noland," he lisped juicily, "you ashked if you had a twin brother?"

"Or *have* a twin. Did I, or do I?"

"Itsh not — that shimple."

"How could it not be *that shimple?*" Nat mocked. "Either I do or do not have a twin brother!"

"When you hear," Gelliard wheezed in staccato bursts, "the whole shtory . . . of your birth . . . and adopshion . . . you will know why I shay . . . itsh not . . . that shimple . . ."

Desperately wanting to know how he came into the world, Nat tethered his temper and listened to the astonishing story.

For the better part of an hour, Gelliard Grimshade sputtered, coughed, and drooled his way though an improbable saga — a lurid Dickensian tale in which the infant Nat had a major role.

Early in Gelliard's recounting of the gruesome events of forty-odd years ago, Nat's jaw dropped, and there it locked for most of the old man's bizarre tale. As his recital neared its end, to Nat's surprise, Sally Grimshade shrieked and ran from the room, sobbing hysterically.

"Now, young man," Gelliard explained apologetically, "you shee why I shaid . . . it wash not . . . that shimple?"

A stunned Nat muttered, "This — isn't true — these — things you've just told me — it can't be true!"

"It ish . . . every lasht word . . . true."

No longer able to control his anger, Nat stood up and pointed an accusing finger at the rotting old man in the wheelchair.

"You are depraved! You belong in prison!" Nat screamed, his voice and body trembling with rage. *"You're a monster!"*

Nat stormed from the house, raced to his waiting limousine, and shouted to the dozing driver, *"Wake up and drive, dammit!"*

On the way to Logan Airport, Nat, his

head filled with graphic descriptions of bloody events and acts of cruelty, stared at the cell phone in his trembling hand.

"Call Glennie," he ordered. "She'll calm you down."

"*You* call her — I'm fucking nauseous!"

"What time is it?"

"Look at your watch!" he screamed.

"I don't have one!"

"*So ask the driver, schmucko!*" he bellowed.

"It's nine-fifteen," the frightened driver answered. He waited a moment. "Sir, are you all right?"

"Am I all right!? How the fuck can you ask if I'm all right? Does this screaming and rude behavior of mine seem all right to you? Damn!"

It was then that Nat knew Dr. Frucht had not cured him of thinking out loud.

"I'm sorry, I didn't mean to yell at you. What's your name?"

"Schmucko is fine," the driver kidded, hoping to calm the weirdo, "but my wife calls me Ed."

"Forgive me, Ed. I've just had a couple of bad hours."

"Sir, there's a bottle of scotch back there — and ice in the cooler — if you feel you, uh, need a . . ."

"Yeah, I need a . . ." Nat said, pouring a double scotch and downing it.

After his second double, and experiencing some blurred vision, he asked, "How about this time on the rocks, Nattie boy?"

"Yeah, the ice'll dilute the alchlo-lo-hole," Nat stuttered, " 'n slow me down — don't wanna get too drunk."

"Right, if the pilot dies — I gotta be a l'il sober — to fly the friggin' plane."

While sipping his fourth double, Nat dialed Glennie.

"I sorry, Señor Noland," Ida, their Nicaraguan housekeeper informed him, "but Madam no 'vailable — she talk *muy importante* phone call on other line."

"Bullshit with her *muy 'portante* phone call, Ida — I got a *more muy 'portante* phone call — right here!" Nat shouted, pointing to his cell phone, then throwing it at his driver. As Nat toppled over on his face, he mumbled, "Shit, missed!" and before passing out he muttered, "More — *mucho — 'portante.*"

The rattled chauffeur picked up Nat's cell phone, checked out his cracked windshield, and prayed that his schizoid passenger would not awaken and do further violence to his life and limo.

10

Los Angeles/London
As Nat stormed out of the Grimshade home, the phone rang in his Bel Air home. Glennie picked it up and heard a man with an English accent ask, "Have I reached the home of the author Nathaniel Noland?"

"You have."

"*The* Nathaniel Noland, the author of *Nadesha*?"

"*Nadesj*da!" she corrected. "Can I help you?"

"Yes, I would very much like to speak with Mr. Noland."

"He is not at home at the moment. May I ask who's calling?"

"Morton Quigley, and I am calling from London. When do you expect him?"

"Not till very late this evening. Why don't you leave your number?"

"How late this evening, would you say? It is rather important."

Probably a pushy fan, Glennie thought, *wanting his book autographed.*

"Perhaps I can help you?"

"Are you related to Mr. Noland?"

"I'm his wife. May I ask the reason for your call?"

"Well, it is a rather, uh, unusual one, Mrs. Noland." He chuckled. "Let me see — where to start. Ah, this morning! Yes, this morning," Morton began, his voice quivering with excitement, "I was caught in a downpour and took shelter in this quaint bookshop — and while there, I bought a gift for my wife — Sarah is addicted to romance novels —"

"— and you found one of my husband's books," Glennie continued impatiently.

"I did indeed. Sitting on the used-book counter was *Nadeesha!*"

"*Nadesj*da!"

"*Exactly.* Sarah loved the gift and she —"

"— she would like for Mr. Noland to autograph it for her?"

"No — well, yes, that would be nice — but —"

"If you'll mail the book to Mr. Noland, and enclose a self-addressed stamped envelope, my husband will be delighted to —"

"That is *not* the reason I called, Mrs. Noland," he said, raising his voice.

"Then what *is* the reason, Mr. Quigley?"

"To inquire if the photo of your husband

on his book jacket is a good likeness."

"That particular photo, which I took," she said, trying to remain civil, "is an excellent likeness."

"In that case, Mrs. Noland" — Morton chuckled — "you have been chatting with your brother-in-law!"

"What the devil are you talking about?"

"Your husband and I are twin brothers!" he shouted gleefully. "And if you give me your e-mail address, I will send you irrefutable proof!"

After giving Morton Quigley their e-mail address, Glennie immediately dialed Nat's cell phone and was shocked to hear a strange voice answer. "Ma'am," the strange voice asked, "are you related to the drunken gent who just threw this cell phone at my head and then passed out in the back of my limousine?"

With calm efficiency, Glennie contacted the proper personnel at the airline, called Nat's physician to arrange for Nat to be put on the plane in Boston, be carried off by paramedics in L.A., and be delivered by a private ambulance to his bed on the second floor of their Bel-Air home.

The following morning a groggy, disoriented Nathaniel Noland awoke, sat up, quickly looked about, and sighed with relief.

That horrendous nightmare I had last night, he thought, *was a dream, a bad, bad dream! There is no Dr. Grimshade — and no horror stories!*

"Good morning, darling,"Glennie sang cheerily as she entered carrying a mug. "I thought I heard you stirring. Ready for your Postum?"

"Not yet," Nat said, his head throbbing. "Honey, I gotta tell you about my nightmare. It was horrible."

"Ah, poor darling — your meeting with Dr. Grimshade must have triggered it."

"My meeting with Grimshade," Nat said, confused. "How do you know about that meeting?"

"I don't. But I'm assuming that you got drunk as a skunk because of something you learned in Boston."

Nat fell back on his pillow and put a hand over his eyes.

"So I didn't dream Grimshade," he moaned. "I met with the bastard. Of course! I called to tell you about it — but Ida said you were talking. Who the hell were you talking to who's more *'portante* than me — than I?"

"Oh, just some English gentleman calling from London," she said, smiling playfully, "to tell you that he's your twin brother!"

104

Nat stiffened and stared at his wife.

"You say he's English," Nat asked, speaking slowly, "and he called from London? What did he have to say?"

Glennie gave him a quick recap of her conversation with the gentleman and then handed Nat the photos he had e-mailed.

"This is uncanny!" Nat yelled, jumping out of bed. "Holy shit! Glennie, I know about this guy — his name is Buddy Keebler!"

"He said his name was Morton Quigley."

"Not Buddy Keebler?"

"Definitely not!"

"He might have changed it to Keebler."

"Darling, are you hallucinating?"

Speaking at a trip-hammer pace, Nat again related the strange and fortuitous meeting he'd had with Dr. Trampleasure, and how she had mistaken him for "this Buddy Keebler cookie." Nat wasn't sure what his motive was in mentioning that Dr. Trampleasure was "very attractive" — or why he added, "If I weren't happily married to the most desirable of all women, this Trampleasure might have a shot at me."

During all this, Nat managed to drink his Postum, get fully dressed, call London, leave his name on Quigley's answering machine, and make back-to-back appointments in Tarzana. Nat was most eager to discuss this exciting new development with Drs. Frucht and Trampleasure.

"What's your guess, Glennie?" Nat asked, referring to the photo. "Married or single?"

"I told you, darling, he bought your book for his wife!"

"Oh, yes." Nat shrugged. "Ah, poor Keebler won't know what he missed out on."

As Nat turned to go, he "missed out on" seeing his wife arch an eyebrow and mutter, "Oh, really!"

As she watched Nat pull out of the driveway, Glennie thought about Nat's drunken dreams and wondered if Dr. Trampleasure might have been in them.

11

Nat was fortunate that he did not have an accident driving to Tarzana. His throbbing head was crammed with a collage of images and thoughts. For the first time in ages, he was finding it difficult to have a substantive conversation with himself. At a traffic light, he attempted to have one.

"So, what do you think?" he said, looking into the tilted rearview mirror.

"About what?"

"About the shit that's happening!"

"What shit?"

"The Grimshade shit!"

"Screw you!"

"Screw you!" Nat yelled, straightening the mirror. *"I can't talk to you!"*

For the remainder of the drive, Nat succeeded in doing something that, of late, he had been unable to do — make his mind a complete blank. It was so successful that he forgot where he was going and drove past his exit ramp.

He offered no apology to Dr. Frucht for

being seven minutes late, and he further surprised the doctor when he walked to the couch and said, "I'd like to do this lying down."

Nat's head was down and he was talking before Dr. Frucht could snatch the used paper doily from the pillow and replace it with a fresh one.

"Doctor, look at this e-mail my wife received last night," Nat said, passing the photo to him.

"Is this a snapshot of you?"

"No!" Nat barked, quickly snatching it back. "But before we talk about him, I've got to talk about me and my trip to Boston — and my experience with this old ghoul of a doctor."

For a good portion of the session, between a flood of tears, wrenching sobs, and jaw-clenching anger, Nat managed to recount what he had learned from Dr. Gelliard Grimshade. As Nat unburdened himself about the circumstances of his birth and adoption, a raptly attentive Dr. Frucht was moved to do two things he normally did not do: take copious notes and allow a session to run into his next patient's time. Nat was in midsentence when the doctor reluctantly announced that they would have to stop.

"Oh, too bad. Tell me, Doctor," Nat asked, tossing a clump of tear-soaked tissues into the trash, "do you think that what I've just told you might explain my nutsiness?"

"Perhaps."

"I take the cake, don't I?"

"Mr. Noland," Dr. Frucht said, standing up, "it may well be that you do 'take the cake'!"

A drained but relieved Nathaniel Noland smiled as he left the doctor's office. He continued smiling as he sat down in Dr. Trampleasure's waiting room.

Damn, I knew it! I am one sick mother! he thought, his smile turning into a chuckle. *A licensed Viennese psychiatrist said that I take the cake!*

Across the hall, Dr. Frucht appeared to be listening intently to Mrs. Chase discuss her problem in finding "a truly competent hairdresser who is also a good colorist" and "the danger of using harsh bleaching solutions on delicate hair." While his patient droned on, Dr. Frucht was thinking about Nat Noland and scanning some of the notes he had jotted down during Nat's emotion-packed session. With his smooth-writing gel pen, he underlined the words "murder" and "triplets."

12

Dr. Trampleasure greeted Nat warmly and apologized for keeping him waiting. Nat, in turn, apologized for calling so early and for being secretive about the reason behind his visit. "This is the reason," he explained, holding up the photo. "Do you recognize this man?"

"Of course," she said, eyeing him curiously. "It's you!"

"No, that is not me. I'll give you a hint," he said slyly. "I received this photo by e-mail last night — from London!"

"London? Oh, my goodness," she said, staring at the photo. "If Buddy Keebler grew up to look exactly like you, Mr. Noland, then Buddy Keebler must be your twin brother!"

"Not necessarily."

"What do you mean, 'not necessarily'?"

"I have no doubt that this man and I are, at least, brothers, but it's moot whether or not he is Buddy Keebler."

"Who in heaven's name could he be?"

"He could very well be who he says he is — Morton Quigley, one of triplets!"

"Are you — a triplet, Mr. Noland?"

"If the information I received in Boston from a drooling madman was accurate, yes, I am one of three."

"I am thunderstruck," she said, shaking her head. "Mr. Noland, if this —"

"Doctor, I prefer you call me Nat."

"And I prefer Gertrude to Doctor."

"Deal. You were saying, Gertrude?"

"If this Morton Quigley isn't Buddy Keebler, might he know where Buddy is?"

"He might. By the way, Morton Quigley is married — if you're interested."

"I am," she said, looking at her hands. "It surprises me that I am — but I am."

"I can give you his number." Nat laughed, hoping to lighten the moment. "Maybe he's not in a happy union."

"Well, I hope he is," she said sincerely. "Well, Mr., uh, Nat —"

"Mr. Nat? Just plain Nat will do fine."

"Well, Just Plain Nat," she joked back, "how is it that you never knew you were part of a multiple birth?"

"Because the details of my birth make up a gruesome horror story," Nat said, wincing, "one that few people knew until this dying, unethical old bastard who engi-

neered it decided to tell all before he shuf-
fled off. Probably to make peace with the
Lord — or his conscience, if he ever had
one."

"You seem to be enraged at this 'unethical
old bastard,'" she said, pronouncing
"bastard" *BAH-stahd,* which made Nat
smile. "Would you care to tell me what exactly he did? It seems to have been something rather unsettling."

" 'Rather unsettling'!" he shouted. "How
about disgusting, immoral, reprehensible,
and fucking illegal? Sorry, Gert — uh, Gertrude."

"Gert is fine. Nat, I'm sorry. I don't have a
right to meddle."

"Yes, you do. You want to find Buddy
Keebler, and I want to find me — and two
other guys like me. We can both help to do
both."

Nat's face flushed, and he suddenly felt a
pang of conscience.

What the hell are you doing, Nat? he
thought. *Are you about to unburden yourself to a stranger, and a strange stranger at
that, an empathologist?*

And what the hell is an empathologist?

*Someone who empathizes! I can sure
use some empathy just about now.*

You could've gotten loads of it from

Glennie — if you had told her about the meeting. Why didn't you take the time to tell her?

Because I didn't have the time!

Nat took a deep breath, apologized to Gert in advance for any language and behavior that might explode from him, and started — or wanted to start, but hesitated.

"Nattie boy," he said, voicing his thought, "just tell the friggin' story!"

"Why don't *you* tell it," Nat said, unaware that he was continuing the conversation.

"Okay, okay!"

"Don't forget to tell about —"

"I was intending to —"

Dr. Trampleasure stared at Nat, trying to guess what he was doing. Could he be using this internal dialogue as a storytelling device? Perhaps it was an author's colorful way of kick-starting his brain.

"Gertrude," he began methodically, "everything I relate to you now came directly from Dr. Grimshade's twisted, drooling mouth. For over an hour I listened to this stroke victim lisp his way though a horror story."

"I hope it won't take you an hour," she said, checking her desk clock.

"I'll boil it down," Nat promised. "To begin, it seems that the Grimshade Adoption Agency and I were spawned within months of each other. Dr. Grimshade and his wife were its founders, and the good doctor, besides running the agency, was also, by his own admission, a very active philanderer. In his long career, he had a total of at least three unsuspecting wives. It seems that my life history began in Houston, where the doctor seduced, raped, and abandoned Lena, a young dancer who was touring with a road company of *The Music Man.* Soon after that one-night stand, Lena learned she was pregnant. Of course, old Dr. Grim*shit* was blissfully unaware of her condition, or of her location — or her last name. But Lena knew his. After losing her job dancing because she started to 'show,' and needing funds, she checked every directory in the United States looking for a Gelliard Grimshade, and finally Boston coughed up Daddy's name. She called to congratulate him on his impending fatherhood — and to ask for financial assistance. Now, this monster, who was in the adoption business, was always looking for babies, and since he had helped create this one, he could get it at a bargain price. To keep his wife from knowing what a shit she had married, he arranged to place Lena in a home for single mothers-to-be — in Portland, Oregon, as far away from Boston as possible. Naturally he was overjoyed when she found out that she was carrying triplets. By the way, my mother's name, I learned after asking him a half-dozen times, was Lomax. Lena Lomax," Nat announced reverently. "Beautiful name, isn't it?"

Nat suddenly whirled and angrily slapped at the back of a club chair. "That dirty bastard!"

"Nattie, calling that *dung ball* a dirty bastard is a compliment!" he shot back.

"And so is calling that *scumbag* a dung ball!"

Gertrude, realizing that Nat was unaware he was talking to himself, gently asked him if he was all right.

"Uh-oh," he answered sheepishly. "Did you just hear me call Grimshade a dung ball?"

"And a scumbag."

"I thought I was getting better." He sighed. "I didn't realize that I was thinking out loud again. You know, that's the reason I see Dr. Frucht."

"No, I didn't."

"Sorry," he said. "Did I scare you?"

"No, but you did surprise me. Please go on."

"Well, she's at the home for six months

and everything is going well, but one night, uh, Lena —"

"Your mother," Gertrude offered.

"I guess I should say 'my mother,' but I find it hard. I've got a perfectly good mother whom I love. Anyway, Lena, my poor birth mother, phones Grimshade, my philandering fuck of a father — I'm comfortable calling him that, if it doesn't offend you."

"It does not."

"Well, she tells the scumbag that the facility is not set up for multiple birthings and will not take responsibility for the babies' well-being. By this time Grimshade has already received substantial fees from three wealthy couples — each couple told of this young, intelligent college sophomore who was taken advantage of by one of her professors and was desperate to find some loving couple to care for her baby — because, and get this, in her seventh month she was blinded in a car accident."

"Nat, did he not consider finding a couple who would take the three babies?"

"That requires sensitivity, which that penurious prick doesn't have. Sorry."

"Please don't be."

"That s.o.b. searched out rich, older clients — ones who had difficulty finding babies. In this case he got three exorbitant fees instead of one. Now comes the ugly part," Nat said, standing up, then sitting down, then standing again, then pacing. And while pacing, he prodded himself, "Nat, get on with it!"

"Okay, okay, the ugly part," he responded testily. "A few days before Lena was due to give birth, Grimshade arrived at the home and was told that she had disappeared. He was furious!"

"She did not want to give up her babies!" Gertrude guessed.

"How did you — ? Of course, you're an empathologist. Lena had called him a month earlier to tell him that she'd had second thoughts about the adoption, but he offered her a bundle of money to give up the kids — which she took. He was sure she would go through with it."

"Where did she go?" Gertrude asked. "Nat, this is a very unnerving story."

"And it gets worse. Less than a half hour before Grimshade showed up — did I say that it was a miserably cold and rainy day?"

"No, but I might have guessed it would be," Gert said, shuddering.

"Boy, Shakespeare had it right: 'When sorrows come, they come not single spies, but in battalions.' Well, in that foul weather, Lena grabbed some keys and drove off in somebody's station wagon. Grimshade figured she'd be driving to the nearest hospital looking for some kind of sanctuary. Well, he figured right. About a mile from the hospital, Grimshade caught up with her on this two-lane road. He actually told me how he forced her to stop by cutting in front of her. As he described it, he got out of his car and stood in this drenching rain, pleading for Lena to lower her window so they could talk, but she refused. Both were shouting at the top of their lungs — he trying to persuade her to get in his car and return to the home, and she screaming about going to a hospital where they'd let her keep her babies! During the argument, Grimshade realized that Lena was in labor."

"Oh, no!"

"Yes!" Nat shouted. "That poor girl was driving herself to a hospital while in labor! Can you believe this?"

"It is hard to imagine —"

"That bastard," he interrupted, "had the gall to say to me that he would never forget that night. He said that he stood there helplessly while she gunned her motor and drove off. He chased her down that rain-slick road — he said that he was getting close, but before he could stop her," Nat said, choking up, "she skidded off the road and plowed into an oak tree. Her head went though the windshield. When Grimshade got to her, she was . . . gone."

Gertrude touched Nat's arm. "How awful."

Nat shook his head and mumbled, "My birth mother . . . never got to meet me."

Nat's whole body shuddered as he looked at Dr. Trampleasure through teary eyes. "And she never got to meet you, Glennie . . . I just called you Glennie, didn't I. Glennie is the one I should be telling all this to."

After a sip of water, Nat calmed himself and went on to describe the gruesome, self-serving decisions Dr. Grimshade made after discovering that Lena was dead and the fetuses' hearts were beating.

Fearing that he'd have to return the money to the couples, Grimshade, to protect his investment, performed a C-section in the back of the station wagon. With the small blade of his pocketknife, he made an incision and extracted three squalling infants, wrapped each in newspaper, transferred them to his car, and drove to the hospital. He called the Portland police and told them the location of the station wagon, inventing the part of how he came upon it and stopped to do the good deed that caused there to be a bloody, eviscerated corpse lying in the backseat. He explained how he did not wish to jeopardize the lives of the three babies by taking the time to load the corpse into his car and bring it to the hospital. When the police detective determined there was no foul play, and that Dr. Grimshade had acted the Good Samaritan, even going the extra mile and overseeing the babies' adoptions, they let him go about his business."

"His lucrative and unsavory business," Gert editorialized.

"You know, Gertrude," Nat said thoughtfully, "even though that villain seemed to be confessing his sins to me by recounting the horrors of my birth night, and doing this mea culpa thing, I felt that he was obliquely asking for my forgiveness, which he will never get. You know, I have this eerie feeling that he was withholding something from me — maybe about my mother."

"Having eerie feelings is quite understandable. Your poor brain has been given too much to process."

"One thing my brain will never process" — Nat groaned — "is accepting that this evil human being is my father!"

13

On leaving Gertrude's office, a guilt-ridden Nat called Glennie on his cell phone and begged for her forgiveness. Knowing her husband's penchant for drama, she did not worry that he had done anything that needed serious forgiving. *Although,* she thought, *whatever it was, it had better not involve the "very attractive" Dr. Trampleasure.*

"Forgive you for what, darling?" she asked.

"I just left Gertrude's office — that is, Dr. Trampleasure's office —"

"Oh? Gertrude and Dr. *Tramp*-pleasure share an office?" Glennie asked, purposefully mangling the name.

"No, honey, she's one person, and it's *Tramp*leasure, Dr. Gertrude Trampleasure. I told you about her. I just spent a half hour with her and —"

"— and you want me to forgive you for that?" she snapped.

"Yes — no, Glennie, not for spending

time with her but for telling her all about my meeting in Boston before I got to tell *you* about it. I'm on my way home. It's a horror story. In the meantime, can you do me a favor?"

"Certainly, darling," she said, sheathing her rapier. "What's the favor?"

"I'd like you to call Gertrude —"

"Me?" Glennie asked, taken aback. "You want — me — to call your Dr. Pleasure?"

"Trampleasure, hon," he corrected, sighing. "And she's not *my* Dr. Trampleasure! Look, just call her and give her Morton Quigley's number — her number is on my night table. She's very anxious to find out if he is Buddy Keebler, or if he knows where the real Buddy Keebler is — she had a thing with him when they were youngsters."

"Nat, slow down," Glennie said, thoroughly confused. "Are you saying that you may be one of three?"

"Yes, I told you I'm a triplet — no, I didn't, and that's why I feel like a shit! I'll be home in forty minutes and tell you everything. Who my father is. Who my mother is — was — and why I'm so screwed up!"

The moment he hung up, Nat wasted no time before engaging in a screaming argument with himself.

"Hey, schmuck, why the hell did you ask

Glennie to give Quigley's number to Gertrude?"

"Because I *am* a schmuck!"

"Why didn't you wait till you got home and give her Quigley's number yourself?"

"Because I'm a *stupid* schmuck!"

"Glennie is pissed!"

"She's got every right to be, hasn't she?"

"Damn right she has!"

"And why did you have to tell Glennie that Dr. Trampleasure is attractive?"

"Because I'm an idiot!"

"Glennie calling her Dr. Tramp was not accidental."

"I know — she's mad at me."

"Can you blame her?"

"No! She may not talk to me when I get home."

"And I wouldn't blame her —"

"I'm a stupid idiot!"

"So am I!"

For the remainder of the drive home, Nat had nothing to say, but his mind was awhirl. He knew there was something different about the high-decibel exchange he had just had — but it surprised and delighted him. A mile or so from his destination, he happily concluded that in that last discussion, his two voices, which were ordinarily discordant, now screamed at each other in agreement.

The major surprise of the long day was waiting for Nat when he returned home. He was expecting a less than welcoming wife but did not imagine that she would totally ignore him. He walked into his bedroom and found her sitting at the edge of their bed holding the phone to her ear. Nat greeted her with a soft "Hi, hon" and received a strange, knowing smile in return.

"Yes, he just walked in," Glennie said into the phone. "Yes, please do, we'll be up for a while — and thank you for understanding. Bye."

A subdued Glennie told Nat that she had been speaking with Dr. Trampleasure and that the doctor might be calling back later that evening.

"Did you give her Quigley's number?" was all a confused Nat could think to ask.

"Yes, minutes after you told me to, and we've been on the phone ever since, and Nat, I must tell you, your Dr. Trampleasure is quite a remarkable person. She is a lovely soul."

"Really?" Nat blinked, trying to focus. "Uh, what led you to that conclusion?"

"Hearing her talk."

"Talk about what?"

"You!"

"Me?"

"Yes, you," she said, reaching for his hand, which he cautiously allowed her to take, "and the conversation you had with her."

"I talked about my trip," Nat said, now more interested than confused. "I told her about Boston —"

"During our phone call," Glennie said, "the most interesting thing Gertrude told me —"

Gertrude? A lovely soul? Nat thought. *The doc's a lesbian and she hit on my wife!*

"— was not so much what you said," Glennie continued, "but what she felt you were *feeling* as you said it."

"What did I say, and what did she feel I was feeling?" Nat demanded.

"Gertrude said that after you related the story of your birth, you seemed tortured by the fact that you hadn't told it to me."

"Well, sweetie, I don't know if I was tortured, but I felt awful. I don't know why I didn't stop to tell you."

"Gertrude felt that as soon as you learned about Morton Quigley's existence, the novelist in you had to race out and track the Buddy Keebler story."

"Some pretty smart empathologizing she did," Nat offered, smiling.

"Nat, I hope you won't be angry, but I asked Gertrude to tell me what she learned from you. She recommended that I wait and hear it from you, but I insisted and she obliged. Was I wrong?"

"No, darling." Nat smiled with relief, hugged her, and whispered, "I'm happy not to have to tell that story again — to anyone — ever!"

Glennie took Nat in her arms and rhythmically rocked him back and forth, thinking, *Poor baby — poor baby —*

That evening, after slipping into bed and pleasuring each other mightily, they reversed their usual pattern, Glennie immediately nodding off and Nat remaining wide awake. His mind racing, he went to his computer, where he reread the last chapter of *NNNNN* and began to write.

The Garden of Civviliaa
Nine Moons Later

On this day of the current moon, the inhabitants of Civviliaa, who now numbered thirty-five, had gathered to watch a male infant spring from the loins of Eluria, sister to Neparia. Cain, who had been very young when he witnessed the birth of Abel, now watched the process with a deeper understanding and compassion. The wrenching pain Eluria endured to pass the struggling infant from her womb was both heroic and worrisome. *Worrisome, to Cain, that his Neparia, now swollen with child, would soon experience long, torturous hours of unrelieved suffering.*

And it came to pass that one moon later, as Cain had feared, all of Civviliaa heard screams and curses, louder and more sustained than any their ears had ever before heard — and their eyes did behold what they had never before beheld. From Neparia, they saw arrive not one but two new lives! Two kicking, crying infants, so alike to each other — but so unalike to their mama or their dada.

All remarked on how strange it was that the skin of the infants was shades darker than the skin of their father — and shades lighter than the skin of their mother and all who did abide in Civviliaa.

As different as was their skin color to all others, so alike to each other were the infants' features that Slama, brother to Neparia and the Leader of Civviliaa, decreed that the infants be entered into the BOOK OF BYRTHS as: Two Worthy Infants in Nature Similar. When referring to his babies, Cain used but the first letters of the entry, Two Worthy Infants in Nature Similar — and thus was born the word T.W.I.N.S.! Before the birth of their T.W.I.N.S., Cain and Neparia each favored a different name for their expected infant, but when two infants did arrive, two names were needed — and so the infants came to be called Kwigli and Keyblah.

Nat was smiling as he crawled into the toasty bed Glennie had warmed with her body for half the night. He was tempted to awaken her to announce that Neparia had given birth to twin boys and that he had named them Kwigli and Keyblah. He also resisted the urge to call and inform Gertrude that, in his new novel, her long-lost love Buddy Keebler lived on as "Keyblah." Glennie did not stir as Nat deftly eased himself into the spoons position, cupping her deliciously warm rear end with his cool thighs. He was congratulating himself on how he had accomplished this without awakening her, when a ringing phone jolted her awake. Seconds later, Nat was jolted to learn from a dispassionate voice on the phone that Gelliard Grimshade had committed suicide.

For what was left of the night, Nat tried to understand how he could possibly be depressed about Grimshade taking his life.

"Tell me, Glennie," he pleaded, "how can I feel a sense of loss about a man I met and hated at first sight? How could I be mourning the loss of that shitty inhuman being?"

"Perhaps it's because that shitty inhuman being," Glennie proposed softly, "was your father?"

"No, the sense of loss I feel," Nat said, rubbing his forehead, "has to do with his not giving me a full debriefing. I know that bastard was withholding something. Something that concerns me. Now I'll never get to know what the hell it was. Damn him!" Nat mumbled, reaching for his socks.

"Nat, where are you going?"

"To find out what that bastard was withholding from me!" he said, struggling to put his socks on.

"Nat, it's six in the morning —"

"Exactly," he said through a yawn, "and the sooner I start looking for the missing pieces of me, the sooner I'll — I'll —"

"You'll what?"

"The sooner I can get some sleep . . ." Nat mumbled, falling back on his pillow. "Don't let . . . me . . . sleep too long . . ."

As Glennie covered him with a blanket, he muttered, "Gotta find Lomax . . . Lena . . . Lena Loma . . . Loma Lena . . ."

14

Sarah Quigley was curled up on the sofa and deeply engrossed in her book when the phone rang for the second time in ten minutes. She had vowed not to allow anything to distract her from finishing the last chapter. She had to know which of the three suitors would capture Nadesjda's heart. If the phone rang again, she was hoping Morton would answer but knew he wouldn't. He never picked up in the middle of his daily workout. Had she not been worried about her granny falling and breaking her other hip, Sarah would not have answered this last ringing.

"Hello," she said curtly.

"Hello, have I reached the home of a Morton Quigley?"

"You have," Sarah answered, relieved that it was not her granny.

"Is Mr. Quigley about?"

Not recognizing the woman's voice, Sarah asked, "May I say who is calling?"

"Gertrude Trampleasure. Nat Noland gave me this number —"

"Nat Noland?" Sarah screeched. "He's my husband's twin brother! I am reading his book — I have it in my hands — I've almost finished it! Is this not an amazing co-incidence? Why did Mr. Noland give you our number?"

"He thought that your husband and I might know each other from school — it is possible that he and I may be good friends — or . . ."

"Or what?" Sarah asked suspiciously.

"Or there is a third person somewhere who looks exactly like Mr. Noland and your husband."

"I don't understand — are you saying that Morton is a triplet?"

"Unless Morton Quigley is not your husband's real name."

"It most assuredly is! What are you suggesting?"

"That he might have changed it for some reason."

"For what reason, and to what would he have changed it?"

"Not *to, from,*" Gertrude corrected. "From Buddy Keebler —"

"Keebler? Did you say Keebler?" Sarah asked. Suddenly she shrieked, "Morton! Morton, pick up the phone — pick up the phone! Pick up — pick up!"

The hysteria in Sarah's voice sent Morton flying off the treadmill.

"I'm here, darling!" he shouted, picking up the phone. "Did Granny fall again?"

"No, Granny is fine. Morton, I have a Gertrude Trampleasure on the phone," she informed him excitedly, "and both she and Nat Noland suggest that you may be someone other than who you are — that is, not Morton Quigley —"

"Calm down, Sarah," he said, catching his breath. "You're making no sense."

"I know. Why don't I let her explain? Miss Trampleasure, this is my husband, Morton."

"Hello, Morton," Gertrude said, unsure whether she wanted Morton to be Buddy.

"Hello, Ms. — was that, uh, Trampleasure?"

"Yes, Gertrude Trampleasure," she said, disappointed that he did not recognize her name. "Please call me Gertrude."

"Ah, Gertrude, I understand you know Mr. Noland, who seems to be my twin."

"Not seems, Morton — I saw your photo, and you and he *are* twins — at *least* twins."

"What exactly are you saying?"

"To get right to it — does the name Buddy Keebler mean anything to you?"

"It does, it does." He laughed. "Since yesterday the name Keebler has meant a good deal to me."

"You are not by any chance Buddy Keebler?" she asked hopefully.

"Oh, heavens no." He chuckled. "But I owe him — saved my life, he did."

"You know Buddy Keebler?"

"Never met the man, but I would love to. Didn't know his first name was Buddy. Do you have any idea how I might get in touch with him?"

"That was going to be my next question, Mr. Quigley. I am terribly confused."

"As was I when I first heard the name Keebler. It's a rather bizarre story."

One that he proceeded to tell.

Morton had just returned from Cairo, where he had been checking out a business opportunity. He had stayed at the Sonesta Hotel, and all had gone smoothly until he was ready to return home. He had promised his wife and daughter, Ceil, that he would be home for the child's ninth birthday party. He had left ample time for his cab ride to the airport, but a sudden rain shower presented a problem. Ordinarily at the Sonesta there were empty cabs at curbside. That day, however, there were no waiting cabs but dozens of waiting guests looking for cabs. He was on the verge of panicking when an unctuous doorman ran up to him, held an umbrella over his head, said, "I'll get that, sir," then picked up Morton's valise and hurried him to a stretch limousine that was just pulling up. The chauffeur apologized for being late, then asked, "Where to, monsieur?" When a bewildered Morton replied, "The airport!," the driver shrugged and repeated, "The airport! *Oui, monsieur.*" Morton had no idea why he was getting this special treatment and did not want to know. To discourage further conversation, he lay back in his seat and closed his eyes. He was struck by the movie-star handsomeness of his French chauffeur and thought, *I should be chauffeuring him.* It was only when they approached the airport and the chauffeur asked, "Do you know when you will be returning, Monsieur Keebler?" that Morton realized he'd been mistaken for some bloke named Keebler.

"I'm not sure," Morton mumbled.

When the driver pressed him by asking, "Tomorrow, perhaps?" Morton answered softly, "Not likely."

While retrieving Morton's valise from the trunk, the chauffeur requested permission to take a day off to visit his in-laws, and Morton magnanimously gave him the whole weekend off.

The grateful chauffeur thanked him profusely and offered a parting "Bon voyage, Monsieur Keebler!"

"Weren't you curious," Gertrude asked, "about why the driver thought you were Mr. Keebler?"

"I assumed it was a case of mistaken identity, but I wasn't going to question my good fortune. You are suggesting — what?"

"Well, here are the facts. According to photos I have of Buddy as a young man, Nat Noland and Buddy Keebler are identical, as are you and Nat, ergo —"

"Ergo, I am —" Morton muttered, slowly processing the information. "Oh, my gracious — I am one of triplet brothers!"

"Yes, and Mr. Keebler is not aware, as you are now, that he has two identical brothers."

"Oh, my goodness, we should, uh," Morton said, shocked and flustered, "we should get in touch with Mr. Keebler and tell him all this — shouldn't we? Now, how do we —"

"I can call the Sonesta Hotel in Cairo," Gertrude jumped in, recognizing Morton's need for help and guidance. "He must have been registered there. I'll get right on it."

Eager to talk to her old buddy Buddy, Gertrude said a hurried good-bye to the shocked Morton Quigley and dialed Information.

15

A Cairo suburb

François Brut tossed his chauffeur's cap onto the passenger seat, hit the play button on his CD, and lustily sang along with Charles Aznavour as he headed home. His home was a furnished two-room apartment over a three-car garage. When halfway there, he phoned his *chérie,* whose actual name was Sherry, to tell her in his charming, French-accented bad English that he could not wait to see her "soft, white, 'nuded' body" lying on his bed. She said that she preferred to see his muscular, bronzed body in her bed, adding flirtatiously, "François, I don't care where our 'nuded' bodies lie as long as they're screwing."

In the midst of their ritual phone-foreplay, François suddenly thought to ask about her husband.

"*Ma chérie,* you have speak with M'sieur Keebler this morning?"

"No, François, I haven't, why?"

"Last night, how he seem to you?"

"Predictable, as always." She laughed. "Why do you ask?"

"Well, he do not talk to me when I pick him up at the hotel — and he wear a suit I not see before ever."

"Ooh, the man finally took a hint and did a little shopping. That's a surprise."

"And the more better surprise, *ma chérie,* is we have two days without him."

"What are you saying, François?"

"He give me *le weekend* off. I tell him I go visit my in-laws. I do not lie, *chérie.*" He chuckled. "You are my wife-in-law, *n'est ce pas?*"

"François, are you telling me that Mr. Keebler is planning to stay at the factory for the weekend?"

"I do not drive to the factory. I drive him to the airport."

"Why?"

"Because he tell me to. He seem a little confused."

"That's his natural state," Sherry snapped. "What else did he say?"

"That he do not know when he come back."

"Oh, my!"

" 'Oh, my'? Why 'Oh, my'?" François said, clicking off Aznavour.

"He may be getting suspicious. François, where was he flying to?"

"He did not tell. I took him to British Airways."

"London! He has been acting weird lately. I think he's met somebody in London."

The lovers agreed that something was not quite right with Sherry's husband, but they had dedicated themselves to a long, glorious weekend of sex, wine, and videotapes and were not about to let a cuckolded husband thwart their plans.

That morning, Sherry gave the household help the day off, so she and François would be free to "do it" in any room they chose. Their idyllic weekend started seconds after François drove up the driveway of the Keebler estate. As per his suggestion, a naked Sherry welcomed her French lover at the front door with drinks in her hands and fire in her belly. By the time they reached her bedroom, their glasses were empty and François had strip-teased off all of his clothes. As they neared the bed, they stopped to kiss, and as their lips touched, a loud ringing cell phone went off in François's trousers, which he had dropped on the stairway. They jumped apart and immediately agreed not to answer the call. When the ringing stopped, they breathed sighs of relief, fell into bed, and started to giggle — but stopped when the phone on the night table rang. Sherry made no move toward it.

"Let it ring. It's probably my husband, calling from the plane. I don't know why," she said coquettishly, "but I don't think he trusts me."

She waited for the answering machine to pick up, and as she suspected, it was her husband. They listened attentively and reacted by giggling, wincing, feigning anger, and sticking out their tongues at each thing Bernard Keebler asked or said.

"Sherry, where are you? And where the hell is François? I just called his cell phone and he doesn't answer. If you hear from him, tell him to call me on my cell phone. He's been very undependable lately, and if he doesn't straighten up, I'm going to have to let him go. You were right about him, Sherry. You never did like him, did you? Smart girl. I don't know when I'll be home, but I'll give you a heads-up. Love ya."

"That bastard," François shouted at the phone. "He say undependable? He want to let me go — because I two minutes late — it was the rain — and I apologize!"

"Don't worry," Sherry promised, pushing him onto her bed and climbing on top of him. "Even though I never liked you, François," she purred, taking his penis in hand, "I will never, never, never, never let you go —"

16

Nat Noland was furious with himself and fought hard not to tell himself how pissed off he was. He had never struck out when it came to doing research. When preparing to write his novel *Nadesjda,* in order to ensure that the dialogue and behavior of her three disparate suitors rang true, he had spent countless hours reading law books, observing brain surgeries, and visiting crematoriums. Now he was frustrated and angry, and to avoid reverting to his schizoid ranting, he barged into Glennie's sewing room and ranted to her.

"How can it be that in 1961," he asked rhetorically, "a girl named Lena Lomax could dance in a touring company of *The Music Man* in Houston, Texas, and there would be no record of her — not in the program, the newspapers, the theater's archives — nowhere!"

"Have you tried Actors' Equity?"

"And AFTRA and SAG and every theatrical agency — in Houston *and* New York.

It's like she never existed."

"Was there a record of a *Music Man* touring company in Houston that year?"

"Yes!"

"And she wasn't listed in the program?"

"No!"

"You checked the names of all the principals, chorus, and understudies?"

"And the choreographer and wardrobe mistress."

"Nat, how about the home for single mothers she ran away from?"

"No record of a Lena Lomax. Probably had her registered under an assumed name."

The pace of their ping-ponging Q and A picked up when Glennie asked, "Sure her name was Lena Lomax?"

"The old man pronounced it 'Lomaxsh.' "

"Sure it was *The Music Man*?"

"Positive!"

"Sure it was Houston?"

"Positive!"

"Did you check other musicals?"

"Hey, hey, that may be it!" he shouted, racing back to his office. "Let that be it!"

Minutes later, Nat was punching the air with his fists and shouting.

"That was it! Glennie, you're a genius! Lena Lomax wasn't in the touring company of *The Music Man* — she was in a church production of *The Sound of Music*! And, sweetheart, do you remember how you scolded me when I referred to my father as a big shit? Well, I was wrong — he was not a big shit. He was the King of Big Shits! Besides getting Lena Lomax pregnant, that turd also knocked up a singer in *The Sound of Music* — a young Catholic girl, Mary Louise Riley. Poor soul was six months pregnant when she committed suicide."

If Nat needed further reason to continue searching for something positive about his heritage, this last revelation about his father did it. With a minimum of discussion, Nat packed an overnight bag, and as per his instructions, Glennie arranged for his flight to Houston, a hotel room, and a meeting with a private detective.

On the ride to the airport, Nat's tentative mastery over his loudmouthed selves suffered a relapse.

"Nat," he shouted suddenly, "did I take the damn laptop?"

"Right here, Nattie," he answered, tapping the computer lying on the seat.

As he sat staring out at the clouds and fretting about finding his birth mother, an impatient Nat thought, *I've got a choice: I* can sit and fret about the shitty hand Lena Lomax was dealt — or I can write about people whose fate I can control.

The Garden of Eden
The Last Morning of Mourning

It was the morning after the night of the twelfth moon — and a sadness enveloped all who lived in the Garden of Eden. Eve wept and Abel sat silent when Adam declared: "For disobeying his father by fleeing his home to search for a specter, I proclaim the period of mourning for Cain be over! I declare him dead! Henceforth, his name may never again be uttered by any who abide in our blessed garden!"

"Must this be ever so, Adam?" Eve pleaded. "Is there not some manner in which he may redeem himself?"

"There is no redemption," Adam roared, "for one whose selfish act did diminish the Family of Man by half."

"By half?" Abel asked. "Father, in the Family of Man, we are four and Cain is but one —"

"Abel!" Adam bellowed. "Didst thou not hear me declare that henceforth it is forbidden to utter thy dead brother's name?"

Eve stepped between Adam and Abel and quietly did explain that Abel knew not *the meaning of "henceforth." Thus did Eve distract Adam from smiting her son and calling him "idiot."*

"Respectfully I offer, Dada, that my dead brother leaving could not have diminished the Family of Man by half."

"If not by half, idiot, then diminished by what?"

"I know not, but soon I shall know, for I am studying Cain's shiny black stones."

Adam did strike a swift blow unto Abel's head and said unto him, "If ever again thou utter thy dead brother's name, it shall be the last name thou ever wilst utter! I pray thou wilst remember this!"

On feeling the blood gush from his nose and mouth and seeing it splash at his feet, Abel swore, "This I will remember!"

"Want to continue?" Nat asked.

"The flight attendant is giving out snacks," he informed himself.

"What'll it be, pretzels or prose — you choose."

"Pretzels."

Nat ate the pretzels, drank a Diet Pepsi, and nodded off.

17

Soon after graduating from Creedmore, Gertrude Trampleasure, then eighteen and rebounding from her painful breakup with Buddy, married twenty-one-year-old Lars Lolafsen. Lars was a good man — kind, attentive, honest, faithful, and a colossal bore. She hoped that he would change — and he did. Each month of their marriage, he became more and more boring. Lars had the rare ability to bore not only her but everyone with whom he had contact; his good looks attracted hordes of unsuspecting victims. His being kind, faithful, and attentive only exacerbated the situation for Gertrude because Lars was always there, always at her side, and always boring — even during their thrice-monthly, four-and-a-half-minute missionary-position sex encounters. At the end of an interminably long year, his presence became physically painful for her. She managed to withstand the blinding headaches, but when her skin, nails, bones, and hair follicles started to throb, she realized that divorce was her only option. Their divorce was boringly civilized, and for Lars it was heaven-sent. Miraculously, within a year he had met and married a woman who was his match.

Gertrude was thinking about her short-lived marriage to Lars while waiting impatiently for the hotel desk clerk to obtain Buddy Keebler's forwarding address. She had not realized how excited she would be at the prospect of speaking with Buddy — and perhaps having him in her life again. Gertrude, who was ordinarily unflappable, felt her pulse quicken when she learned that "Mr. Keebler had lunch in our hotel dining room yesterday, but we do not have his address."

"May I speak with the maître d'?" Gertrude asked, hoping he would know how to contact Buddy.

"Mr. *Buddy* Keebler? I know of a Mr. *Bernard* Keebler. Might he be that man?" the maître d' said.

By accurately describing Nat Noland, Gertrude convinced the maître d' that Buddy and Bernard Keebler were one and the same, and so obtained Bernard Keebler's business address and phone number. As Gertrude dialed his number, she thought, *Bernard? I can't call him that.*

147

Everybody called Buddy, Buddy.

A secretary answered and informed her that Mr. Keebler was not in, and balked when Gertrude requested Mr. Keebler's home phone number. She relented only when Gertrude, using her professional empathologist voice, identified herself as "*Dr.* Trampleasure, an old and dear colleague."

When the phone rang at the Keebler house, François was about to join his *chérie* in her oversize marble tub but instead grabbed a towel and switched off the Jacuzzi.

François thought, *Damn! If this is M. Keebler say he is coming home, I lose a boom-boom bath with* ma chérie.

Happily, the voice on the answering machine was not Bernard's but a low-pitched, seductive female voice. Her message intrigued François and angered Sherry.

"Hello, Buddy, or should I call you Bernard? This is Gert — I trust you remember me. It's rather important that I talk with you — and soon. Please call me — Gertrude Trampleasure, and my phone number is —"

"Take the number down," Sherry ordered, and François jotted it down.

"Trampleasure, is it? I'll bet that's the

tramp he flew to London to boff!" Sherry ranted. "That damn liar didn't go to any factory this weekend! *François, drop that towel and get in here. Show that bastard how it's done! Let's go — let's go, FRANSWAAAAAAAAAAAAAAAAHH!*"

With the last syllable of his name reverberating off the marble walls, François lowered himself into the tub and did as he was told.

18

Nat was encouraged by two positive signs. On the flight to Houston, he was able to add two acceptable pages to *NNNNN*, and at the Lancaster Hotel, a meeting was scheduled with Jack Craquer, the founder and chief operative of the Cracker Jack Detective Agency.

"I apologize, Mr. Noland," Jack Craquer said, handing Nat a card. "My wife came up with the name — she thought it was clever."

"It's very clever," Nat lied.

What Nat did think clever was the detective's resourcefulness in tracking down a promising lead.

Jack Craquer turned to Nat as they drove through one of the least desirable sections of town and warned him to be prepared for the possibility of learning something disturbing about "this Lena Lomax person we're investigating." Nat could not envision learning anything more disturbing than what he had heard from Grimshade.

Jack Craquer parked his highly polished fifteen-year-old Honda Civic in front of a crumbling three-story clapboard house. Nat eyed the wreck and sighed.

"Pretty dilapidated," the detective agreed, "although, you know, with a fresh coat of paint, this could look —"

"— like a freshly painted dilapidated house."

Nat's apology for making a stupid joke was aborted by Jack's explosive laughter.

"Now, that was damn funny — freshly painted dilapidated house!" he roared.

Nat blanched as he spied a man looking down at them from an open window on the second floor, and he wondered how much the man had heard.

Obviously he had heard it all. "You don't want to paint this dilapidated place. Tear it down," he called out. "I got it listed at one million two — but I'll take an offer," he added good-naturedly. "You dudes looking for me?"

"We are," Jack shouted back, "if you're John Lomax."

"I am. You that Cracker Jack fellow?" he said, leaning out the window. "And is that the gentleman who needs information?"

"Yes, Mr. Lomax," Jack answered. "This is Mr. Noland. Can we come in?"

151

"You gonna ask me personal stuff, Mr. Noland?"

"I guess so," Nat said, smiling nervously.

"I hear you're a writer. Is what I tell you gonna end up in a book?"

"I'm not here looking for book material —"

"Well, whatever you're doin', let's do it up here. Knock on the door — the young lady will let you in."

"Mr. Noland, I'll wait in the car," Jack Craquer suggested. "I'll let you and Mr. Lomax have your, uh, delicate conversation by yourselves."

Our delicate conversation? Nat thought. *Delicate conversation about an expectant mother crashing and dying in a ditch — and a madman-rapist-doctor slicing open her dead body to deliver and sell the triplets he fathered?*

If Nat needed anything to add to the emotional state, he got it when he was greeted at the door by a lovely young African-American woman who introduced herself as Lena Lomax. Walking up the flight of stairs beside her, Nat's mind raced to make sense of this unexpected twist in his already twisted life story.

Maybe, he thought, *this tall, stately*

young woman was named after my mother — because —

Because her mother was my mother's best friend — and danced in the same chorus —

Or maybe she's related to my mother. Yes, she's related to her!

Yeah, that's more dramatic — more controversial — and more likely!

Whoa, whoa, Nat! If she is related to my mother — you know what I am? I am an African American! And I just wrote about Cain and Neparia, a racially mixed couple, having racially mixed twins!

Wow, unfrigginbelievable!

"It's life imitating art! That's what it is!" Nat screamed, too emotional to realize he was laughing and screaming out loud. "It's Life imitating Art!"

"Mr. Norton, I think the phrase is 'Art imitating life,' " Lena Lomax corrected politely.

Before a red-faced Nat could explain himself, a voice from above cried out, "The young lady is right. Art imitates life — not the other way around. Lena's a graduate of the Houston College of Fine Arts. Listen to the lady!"

Using a cane, John Lomax, a light-skinned, hazel-eyed African American, made his way to the landing, where he waited to greet the stranger whose discomforting questions he knew were bound to be bring tears to his eyes one more time. But John Lomax had learned to live with pain. He had lost a foot in Vietnam and had, as he put it, "been living quite *un*comfortably on my government disability check."

In the extraordinary hour Nat spent with John, Nat learned that the internal conversation he'd had with himself while mounting the stairs was pretty accurate: His life was imitating his art. He had not yet come to terms with the fact that he had entered this house as a Caucasian and would leave as "a man of color." How to think about and handle this revelation?

I got me some good parents! he thought. *Without knowing that I, their adopted son, was black, they marched for civil rights and fought for racial equality. That's pretty cool.*

Seated in their meagerly furnished apartment and sipping the ice water Lena had served him, Nat listened intently as John Lomax spoke.

"Lena Lomax was my daughter," he volunteered. "And this young lady sitting at your side is my niece who was named after her. My daughter, Lena, died forty-one years ago — in Portland, Oregon," John

Lomax explained. "Burned up in a car crash — some doctor who was an eyewitness called and said that there was no body to bury — I never found out how she got to Portland — last I heard from her — she was in a show," John continued in his slow verbal shorthand. "Lena was something — full of life — beautiful dancer — a sunny-smiley girl whom God chose not to smile upon. Don't know why — she never missed church on Sunday — her mama didn't either — I did — never went." John stopped and shook his head sadly. "Maybe the Lord was mad at me and took it out on Lena — and on her mama, Mary — my wife — Lord took Mary seven years ago. She was a beautiful woman — Lena took after her. Mary was half Scotch, half Irish, and half English." John smiled. "That's how she said it — when she was funnin' — but when Lena was born, Mary told how 'that baby is half Scotch, half Irish, half English, and half African, which makes her two hundred percent American!' "

All the while John Lomax was talking, Nat worried that John would ask why he was interested in Lena. Nat wrestled with the need to tell John Lomax the whole, ugly truth — which included her seducer's identity and the reason and manner Lena had died in

Portland, Oregon. As a novelist, Nat had thought he could weave events that led up to Lena's death into a nonviolent fairy tale with a bittersweet ending, but so far he had found no way to do that, and until he could find a gentle way to tell the story, he could not tell John Lomax that he was the grandfather of triplet grandsons and that he, Nat Noland, was one of the triplets.

As Nat stood up to leave, the dreaded question about Lena had not been asked, and he breathed a sigh of relief — prematurely.

"Mr. Noland, I didn't ask you why you are interested in Lena. I expected that you would tell me, but I see now that you are leaving . . ."

"Oh, I'm sorry. I didn't tell you, did I? I — I assumed that Mr. Craquer filled you in on that," Nat blathered on lamely. "An old friend of mine knew an old friend of Lena's, and she heard I was going to be here — and she wondered if I could help her find Lena. I'm a writer, and she knew I was good at tracking down information."

"Well," the old man said with a sigh, "I wish you had been able to track down happier information for your friend."

"As do I," Nat said, shaking John Lomax's hand. He thanked John for his time and promised that he would hear from him again, a promise Nat intended to honor.

Nat tapped Jack Craquer's shoulder to awaken him, then climbed into the passenger seat and asked him to drive to the hotel.

"How did it go?" Jack asked, yawning.

"I got what I came for. Let's go!"

"Wait a second!"

"No waiting a second — let's go!" Nat argued.

"Let's just sit for a second!" Nat insisted, then sat back and listened to the angry conversation in his head.

What the hell are you doing, Nat?

I'm going back up there!

Nat, you do what you want. I'm going to the hotel.

Why, Nattie?

Because that man up there is my grandfather and I'm not going to break his heart by telling him that his daughter was raped and sliced up by a monster!

His daughter is my mother and my heart didn't break. It hurt, but it didn't break.

Alarmed by the strange contorted look on Nat's face, Jack Craquer suggested they drive back to the hotel.

Nat did not answer as his internal conversation continued.

Well, Nat, maybe you're stronger than me —

It's stronger than I! And what you are is weaker than I! And dumber. I'm going back up!

And I'm staying here!

"Stay! I'm going back up!" Nat shouted, getting out of the car. "I don't need you!"

"I agree, Mr. Noland, I'd just be in the way," Jack Craquer answered, unaware that Nat was talking to his alter ego. "I'll be right here when you're ready to go. How long will you be?"

"As long as it takes," Nat yelled back as he walked off.

John Lomax, who had been looking out the window, was not surprised to see Nat climbing the stairs. After looking into Nat's eyes and observing his demeanor, he had sensed that Nat was carrying a burden that he was eager to put down somewhere. "Did you forget something, Mr. Noland?"

"Yes, I did, Mr. Lomax. For reasons I'd rather discuss some other time, I chose not to tell you the truth about why I was searching for your daughter. I was wrong not to, and for that I apologize."

At this juncture, Nat felt comfortable enough to tell John Lomax about his being adopted, his need to go to a psychiatrist, his

158

fortuitous meeting with Dr. Trampleasure, and how he first learned that a woman named Lena Lomax might be his mother. John sat motionless and quietly accepted the news that the man who was telling him this was his grandson, someone he never before knew existed. Nat knew he would have to tell the gruesome climax to Lena's story, and he also knew that he was going to sugar-coat the tragic last chapter of her life — and he did it well. Nat felt no compunction about fudging some of the facts about Lena, but he hated himself for depicting Dr. Gelliard Grimshade as the Good Samaritan who came upon a crash site and stopped to minister to a woman who was in labor and near death. Nat described how this skilled surgeon heroically delivered triplets from the young woman before she expired. Because he could not come up with an acceptable lie about John's daughter's last hours, Nat focused on the revelatory news that two of Lena's three children, John's grandchildren, who were unaware of each other, would soon be in contact. Nat was saddened by how seemingly unemotional John was about the news that he had three grandchildren. It soon became clear what John had been focusing on and where his heart was.

"Is it true, Mr. Noland, what that kind

doctor told me?" John asked. "That there was an explosion and Lena burned up in the car — and there was no, uh, body, nothing to bury?"

Nat realized that he could actually answer that question truthfully.

"I don't know, Mr. Lomax, but that's what I heard."

I heard it from you, Nat thought, *and I don't know if it's true, but knowing the kind doctor, I'd guess it's a rotten lie.*

Nat dialed home and hoped his wife was in. He had thought of a cute way of telling her about his historic meeting with John Lomax.

"Hey, honey, when you were in college," he asked, trying to sound casual, "didn't you tell me that you used to date a black guy?"

"Nat, where are you?" his worried wife asked. "Have you been drinking again?"

"Nooo. You did, didn't you?"

"I did not date him — I was engaged to him, you know that. Why, are you . . . ? Oh, my goodness." She laughed, then barreled on, stopping only for corroboration. "John Lomax is black! And he's what? Your uncle? Grandfather? He's Lena's father! Hah, I married an African American after all!"

Hearing the joy and excitement in his wife's voice brought a lump to Nat's throat. If ever Nat had any thoughts about not having married the right woman, they were dispelled forever. *You picked yourself a winner,* he told himself.

"Oh, Nat, why didn't you call and tell me? This is wonderful news! You've got yourself a grandpa. What's he like?"

"He seems nice enough — no, he's *very* nice — good-looking, too — but I don't think either of us has processed what this new development will do to our lives."

"How much time did you spend together?"

"Just long enough to find out who he is and who my mother was. I did notice that the color of his eyes was sort of like mine — and there were some similarities in our chins and cheekbones."

"That's so wonderful! Nat, did he show you any pictures of your mother?"

"No. I don't know if he has any."

"Didn't you ask?"

"No, I was too busy sanitizing Grimshade's gory account of her last day. I didn't want to hang around for the tough questions."

Glennie then surprised Nat by suggesting that he remain in Houston for at least one more day to visit with his grandfather. "Get to know him," she urged. "Take him out to a restaurant — let him find out what a fine and talented grandson he has."

Nat agreed with all her reasons for staying an extra day, but the strongest was one he felt when he left the old house. He had wanted to hug his grandfather, but for fear of rejection, he'd done nothing. Next time, he vowed, whether the old man wanted it or not, he was going to be hugged.

19

A Cairo suburb

Ordinarily Bernard Keebler would have been furious to find that his limousine was not waiting for him curbside, as per his explicit instructions.

"Where the devil is my car, Dano?" Bernard asked.

"It was here, Mr. Keebler," answered the bewildered doorman. "Luis helped you with your bag, and then you drove off."

"I didn't drive off — and I don't have a bag! And now I don't have a ride."

"I'm sorry, Mr. Keebler, but I don't know what happened."

"Well, find out! Meanwhile, I need transportation!" Bernard barked.

"Yes, Mr. Keebler. I'm sorry, Mr. Keebler."

"Mr. Keebler?" a voice rang out. "Are you *Buddy* Keebler?"

Bernard turned toward the voice and shook his head in disbelief. Ten feet away stood a striking woman who at first glance looked vaguely familiar, and on second glance looked like a wish come true.

"Nobody's called me Buddy for twenty years," a broadly smiling Bernard informed the raven-haired apparition slinking toward him, "but I am hoping that you are who I'm almost sure you are."

"Almost sure?" she purred as she wrapped her right leg around his buttocks. "How about now, Buuudddyyy?"

"I'm positive!" He laughed. "Only Laylah Leadbeller ever hugged me with one of her gorgeous legs."

"I am not now Laylah Leadbeller, but I will be again when my divorce from Mr. Wrong becomes final." She giggled and tightened her leg hold on him.

Bernard, who years ago had forgotten how to be playful, wrapped his right leg around her spectacular rear and shouted, "How the hell are you?"

Bernard Keebler was unconcerned that people were staring at him, he was that happy to see Laylah. So happy, he allowed himself to French-kiss his old flame with the passion and exuberance of his youth. To acknowledge the group of approving bystanders who were laughing and applauding their efforts, the lovers reluctantly unsheathed their tongues and shouted, "Thank you! Thank you!"

"Buddy, if you need transportation," Laylah said, throwing kisses to their fans, "I can transport you."

"Laylah, you have already transported me!" He smiled. "But I could use a ride to my factory."

"You've got it," she said, pointing to a red Ferrari. "This okay?"

"It'll have to do." He grinned as he slid into the passenger seat.

The Keebler Toy Factory was exactly sixty kilometers from the hotel, but at two kilometers they passed a charmless roadside inn, properly named the Roadside Inn. They agreed that it looked like the perfect place to stop and have a quick "get-reacquainted drink."

To ask and answer the dozens of personal questions they had for each other, they decided that the inn's executive suite would be infinitely more comfortable than the cramped front seat of the Ferrari. As soon as they were alone, they sat down on the king-size bed that took up most of the suite and started to examine their present life situations. As these two kindred spirits were baring their souls to each other, they were simultaneously baring their bodies.

So comfortable were they together that after an hour of the kind of athletic sex they both had dreamed about long after their Creedmore days, they actually fell asleep in each other's arms.

While Laylah slept on peacefully, Bernard awakened and phoned the foreman of his factory to say that he would not be coming in today, and then, curious to learn what had happened to François, called his home to check his messages. He learned nothing about François, but when he heard the first recorded message, he literally fell to the floor. So shocked was he to hear Gertrude Trampleasure's voice that he sat down a foot short of the chair.

"It's rather important that I talk with you soon" was the phrase that sent him reeling. Twenty years earlier, Gertrude had said something similar to him. It was the night before he split from Laylah — the beautiful, forgiving Laylah, who was now sleeping blissfully not three feet away. Bernard shuddered and looked about to see if there was some alien force in the room guiding his destiny.

How could this be? he thought. *How could the two great loves of my life be in my life again? Are the gods toying with me?*

He had an urge to wake Laylah and share this netherworld experience with her but decided that he had better sort out his feelings before soliciting advice from an interested party. He thought of his wife, Sherry, and recognized the uncanny timing of meeting Laylah and hearing from Gertrude when he was having second thoughts about his marriage. He could not say that he and Sherry were unhappily married, nor could he say that they were happily married — they were simply married. He thought, *Is that enough reason to divorce someone?*

He decided it was, but thought it prudent to wait till morning and see if he still felt about Laylah as he did now — and more importantly, how Laylah felt about him. As he contemplated this, a niggling thought popped up: *What about Gertrude?* A millennium ago, he had betrayed Laylah to be with Gertrude, and he had felt godawful about it. Dare he call Gertrude? He remembered how very beautiful and exciting she was.

What if I am tempted to betray Laylah again? he thought. *It won't happen! At least I can't imagine it happening again. I won't call her, that's it — not now, anyway.*

Bernard was certain of but one thing: His life as he knew it was over.

"Laylah," he whispered, kissing her forehead, "guess who I just heard from?"

An hour passed before Laylah awoke, nudged her sleeping lover, and replied, "I don't know, Buddy. Who did you hear from?"

"Gertrude — Kent —" he mumbled in his sleep.

"What did she want?"

"I — don't know," he added, yawning. "She said — to call her —"

"Where's the number?"

Before falling back to sleep, he muttered, "In my pocka . . ."

Laylah translated "pocka" as pocket, and that was where she found the number. She sat by the phone, remembering the hurt she had suffered when she lost Buddy and trying now to determine whether calling Gertrude was the wise thing to do.

Perhaps, she reasoned, *had I talked things out with Gert and told her how I felt, things might have worked out differently.*

Laylah started to dial, then returned the phone to its cradle. Worrying that Buddy might wake and be irked that she had gone through his pockets, she used the phone in the bathroom. She had to know what Gertrude was up to.

A sleepy Gertrude answered the phone

and, on hearing Laylah Leadbeller's voice, jumped out of bed and squealed with delight.

"Laylah, for goodness sakes — what a wonderful surprise! How are you?"

"I'm really fine, Gert, and what are you up to?" Laylah asked pointedly but pleasantly.

"Working hard and enjoying it. This is so amazing. I've been thinking about you and wondering how you were," Gertrude said, genuinely happy to be speaking to her old classmate. "Laylah, where are you calling from?"

"From Cairo."

The blood drained from Gertrude's face.

"Cairo?" Gertrude asked. "Now, that is a major coincidence. Did you know that Buddy Keebler is in Cairo?"

There was a five-second delay before Laylah answered, "Yes, he's asleep in the bedroom."

There was a seven-second delay before Gertrude asked, "Are you and Buddy married?"

"No, but we're hoping to be," Laylah said, to discourage any predatory thoughts her old nemesis might be having.

"Well, I guess congratulations are in order."

"Thank you. Uh, Gertrude, why did you call Buddy?" Laylah asked. "He told me you called."

"Not to steal him from you, Laylah," Gertrude assured her, the empathologist in her at work. "I called to give him an amazing bit of news."

"About you?" Laylah asked suspiciously.

"No, about him," Gert said coyly.

"What about him?"

"Laylah, it seems that your husband-to-be is one of three identical triplets."

Laylah screamed, Gertrude laughed, and Bernard woke with a start. For the next half hour Gertrude gave Buddy all of the details she knew, plus the phone numbers of his siblings. By the time they hung up, all the old tension between the former lovers was gone and honest civility had taken over.

20

From the time he left John Lomax's apartment until the plane leveled off at its designated altitude, two phrases went through Nat's brain in a continuous loop: *Life imitating art!* and *Art imitating life!* Before the flight attendant had finished announcing that it was safe to turn on electronic devices, Nat had already booted up his laptop and was checking the last line he had written on the flight to New Orleans.

Not too shabby, Nat thought, *but where do I go from here?*

Nat stared at a blank page for a moment and wrote:

Betwixt Eden and Civviliaa

In the four moons since their birth, the T.W.I.N.S. had doubled in weight, and whosoever did look upon Kwigli and Keyblah was impressed by the robustness of their bodies and the width of their smiles. It was evident to all that Neparia was a caring mother and Cain a loving and protective father. For this and for bringing into the world the first Two Worthy Infants in Nature Similar, Slama the Leader did honor the Loving Mates, Cain and Neparia, by bestowing upon them the "Mates Importantes Medallion," the first Civviliaan award ever given.

So elated was Cain by this honor that he could think of nothing but a triumphant return home, where he would share these miracles with his parents.

And so, with the T.W.I.N.S. in their arms and the Mates Importantes Medallions hanging from their necks, Cain and Neparia set out for the Garden of Eden.

When the family reached the valley adjacent to Eden, they stopped for Neparia to suckle the infants and for Cain to collect water. It was when Cain was thus occupied that Abel, who had climbed high up a tree to pick its fruit, did spy his brother and his family. Fearful of his father's wrath, Abel said nothing to him about Cain's presence outside the garden but did inform his grieving mother of her son's imminent return.

And Eve did smile for the first time since Adam had declared Cain dead. And Adam, who had not had his sexual needs satisfied without physically overpowering her, was now hearing a seductive Eve whisper, "Take me for as many comings as it pleases thee."

Eve had hoped that a tired, contented Adam would soften and allow for the redemption and return of his firstborn — but it was not to be.

Dawn broke, and whilst the three inhabitants of Adam's garden did sleep, Cain and his family made their way up the steep hill that led home.

It was Kwigli and Keyblah crying for their mama's teats that awoke Eve, who thought she had dreamed of a baby crying. So real were the cries that Eve left Adam's side to search for the crying infant.

The beat of Eve's heart quickened as she beheld the first woman she had ever seen. On seeing her son Cain smiling proudly, Eve knew all. This beautiful dark woman who nursed a baby on each of her breasts was she for whom Cain had searched.

What Eve could not fathom was how Cain had fathered two babies in the few moons he had been away. So excited and happy was Eve to behold Cain that she paid little note to the unusualness of her son's sons and their mother. But not so Adam, who stood nearby, glowering at his banished son and ignoring all else. Eve exhorted Adam to look upon the beautiful robust infants. Upon hearing the names of the infants and their mother, Adam did become enraged.

"Dear God," he shouted heavenward. "What manner of names are Kwigli, Keyblah, and Neparia? And from what manner of mother were such infants born? And why is the mother's skin like the color of night? And how is it that she suckles two infants of the same age?"

When Cain attempted to answer, Adam said unto Eve, "Since my firstborn no longer exists, thou shalt hear the whispered answers and repeat them!"

When Eve relayed all that Cain had whispered to her, Adam rebutted each of Cain's answers at the top of his lungs.

"I DO NOT ACCEPT THAT: Kwigli and Keyblah and Neparia are proper names. THERE EXIST NO OTHER NAMES BUT ADAM AND EVE AND ABEL! — save for one other, which cannot be uttered.

"I DO NOT ACCEPT THAT: It be possible for two infants to arrive from one belly — on the same day!

"I DO NOT ACCEPT THAT: There exist such unnatural colors of skin as are displayed by the mother and her improperly named infants.

"I DO NOT ACCEPT THAT: He whose name may not be uttered is now present in the Garden of Eden!

"I HEREBY DECLARE THAT: I am dreaming that my sacred abode is being visited by the uninvited and unwanted, and when I awake, all who are present in my nightmare will be gone!"

Then did Adam lay his racked body on the ground and set about to undream his dream. And when he awoke, the uninvited and the unwanted were gone — and so too was Eve.

And so it came to pass that while Adam did spend his days and nights cursing and bewailing his lot, Eve did spend her days loving and helping to care for her GRAND T.W.I.N.S. and her nights being a loving companion to tall, dark, handsome Guffama, older brother to Slama.

Nat typed the last sentence as the flight attendant announced, "Please return all seats to the upright position." He closed his laptop and thought, "*Lying with the tall, dark, handsome* Guffama"? *I can do better than that.*

Yeah, something a little more romantic. How about Romeo?

Too on the head.

Anagram it.

Romeo-um-Omero?

Possible.

Moreo?

You're getting there.

Mooreo?

Mooreo — *that's it! Eve spends her nights being a loving companion to tall, dark* Mooreo! *Good! A loving dark-skinned companion!*

Nat smiled. *Deal with that, Adam!*

21

In the executive suite of the Roadside Inn, Bernard Keebler and Laylah Leadbeller enjoyed three intense hours of enlightened conversation and adulterous sex, after which they made a binding commitment to love each another forever. It was at that moment that Bernard decided the time had come for him to start divorce proceedings.

"Laylah, darling, I don't know how to thank you for giving me the strength to take this step — and the sooner I take it, the better," he said, reaching for his shorts. "Get dressed! We are driving to my home right now to undo the stupidest thing I ever did: saying yes when Sherry proposed marriage."

Laylah balked at the idea of accompanying him, but Buddy convinced her that it was her loving presence that gave him the resolve to do what he must do.

"Buddy," she demurred, "I'd much prefer to wait in the car —"

"And I want you at my side," he said, kissing her cheek, "tonight and forever."

Bernard was not quite sure why, but before arriving at his home, he thought it would be a good idea to call and leave another message, saying that he would not be home till the following morning.

Sherry and François listened to that message while they were deciding whether to loll in the tub or have a little snack. The decision was made for François when the Viagra he had taken earlier did what it was advertised to do. As per Sherry's request, François turned up the volume on Yves Montand singing "St. Germain des Pres," making it difficult to hear anyone opening or closing the front door.

On entering, Bernard might have called out "I'm home, Sherry!" had he not seen the limousine parked in the driveway and François's clothes strewn about the foyer and stairway. Bernard escorted a reluctant Laylah to where the music was playing and, without warning her that it was the bathroom, flung the door open. Bernard was rather pleased to see what he saw: grounds for divorce! Laylah was appalled but mesmerized by the sight of the copulating couple splashing about in the tub. Bernard debated whether to disturb them before they came to orgasm or to wait until he and Laylah were noticed. Between Yves Montand's singing and Sherry's shrieking instructions to François, they might never have been noticed. It was when François obeyed Sherry's in-the-heat-of-passion instruction "Get off me and be a poochie!" that François caught sight of his audience and froze — which provoked Sherry to shout, "Don't stop! Why are you stopping?"

"Because, darling," Bernard explained quietly, "François is a gentleman, and he knows how impolite it is to diddle his employer's wife while his employer is in the room watching him."

Sherry screamed, "Fuck you!," threw a bar of soap at her husband, and ducked under the water. When she surfaced, Bernard calmly told her that she would be getting a call from his lawyer. A cowering and naked François yammered an apology and an explanation about his chauffeuring an "imposter" to the airport. "I swear, M'sieur Keeblere," he stammered, "zis man is a perfect twin of you — he was, how you say — your shitting image."

Bernard thanked François for the information and then fired him, and with Laylah on his arm, walked briskly out of the bathroom — and into a new life.

22

"Driver, without breaking any speed laws, is there a way to get me home faster?"

"I could get off the highway, Mr. Noland, and take the city streets."

"Do it."

Nat could not wait to discuss with Glennie all that had happened to him in Houston. He decided not to phone her. The details of his extraordinary two-day visit with his maternal grandfather warranted a face-to-face debriefing. He was eager to see his wife's reaction to the photos of her new in-laws that had been taken at the dinner he'd hosted at Restaurant Charivari. Nat studied the group photo that included himself, his grandfather, John's niece Lena, two great-uncles, Roy and William, five cousins, and his chatty, white-haired, one-hundred-and-four-year-old great-great-aunt, Harriet Beecher Slaw. As Nat noted the gradations of color in the faces of his new relatives, he thought, *Like it or not, these people's fe-*

male forebears must have received a lot of loving attention from their slave masters.

"Nattie, these people's forebears are," he mumbled, then shouted, *"your people's forebears!"*

"My people's what?" the driver asked fearfully.

"I'm sorry, I'm sorry — I have this psychological thing."

He was disappointed to learn that he was still speaking his thoughts but delighted to discover that he could unashamedly discuss his problem with a stranger.

"I'm seeing this Viennese analyst about it," Nat admitted. "I think another few visits and I'll have it beat."

With this cleansing confession to a limo driver and his discovery and acceptance of his roots, Nat felt as if someone had validated his birth certificate. By the time he arrived home, he was feeling good about himself, something he had not allowed himself to feel for a long time. He did not, however, feel good about seeing three strange cars parked in his driveway.

Shit, he thought. *Glennie's two brothers and their families.*

Today of all days, Nat needed to be alone with his wife, to sort out myriad personal feelings. First among many was their getting used to the fact that he was no longer a Caucasian but "a man of color."

Hey, he thought as he stepped out of the limo, *Alexandre Dumas, my favorite author when I was a kid, was a man of color.*

Nat gave his driver a generous tip and apologized again for scaring him. He checked the cars as he walked to the house, mumbling, "Who the hell do these belong to?"

Glennie, who always found giddiness to be an unattractive trait, nonetheless became certifiably giddy when she saw her husband's limo pull into their driveway. She sounded like a teenager when she popped her head into the living room and shouted, "He's here! Nat's here! I'd better warn him that you're all here. I don't want to risk his having a heart attack."

Glennie met Nat at the door and tried to welcome him with a kiss while he was asking about the cars in the driveway.

"Darling," she said, grinning from ear to ear, "guess who's in the den?"

"Your brothers and their loved ones?"

Having gotten the almost perfect straight line, Glennie shouted, "No, Nat, *your brothers* — and *their* loved ones!"

Nat, who had been thinking about this

moment for the past few days and wondering when it would come and how he would feel when it came, now knew. He would feel nervous, nauseated, and numb.

"They're in the den, right?" he asked, taking his wife's hand. Glennie opened the door and there, standing shoulder to shoulder, were the other two thirds of him, Morton Quigley and Buddy Keebler. They were smiling the same broad, toothy smile and looking at him with four identical hazelgreen eyes. Then, with the precision of an army platoon carrying out a drill sergeant's order, their broad smiles became quivering lips and their hazelgreen eyes filled with tears, propelling them into an emotionally charged three-way embrace, one that Nat later dubbed "The Hug That Broke the Family's Back!" or "The Hug of Hugs." They stayed tightly locked in this weeping phalanx for minutes and might have remained longer had not Glennie asked, "Would anyone care for a glass of chardonnay or some scotch?"

The triplets continued to blubber as their hands shot up and in unison they ordered, "Scotch!"

The sobbing Glennie, the tearful Laylah, and the weepy Sarah Quigley preferred the chardonnay. A sad-faced Gertrude asked for water. She was noticeably affected by the high emotional content of this reunion. Ordinarily she had been able to keep a tight rein on what she considered excessive outbursts of emotion, but not today. Through wet eyes she looked with envy at Glennie, wed to Nat — Sarah, wed to Morton — and Laylah, to be wed to Buddy. What made her most sad was that she sincerely believed Laylah and Buddy were a perfect match. Two glasses of chardonnay later, Gert told them so, which moved Laylah to throw her arms about her old archenemy and thank her a dozen times for being "so gracious, so sweet, and a real, real friend."

Glennie had correctly envisioned that the thrust of the evening would be the asking and answering of questions that the three brothers would have for one another, and particularly the questions that only Nat could answer. She discussed with him the practicality of having dinner before they got into the "heavy memories," but Nat felt that neither he nor his brothers could eat anything until they sat and talked for a bit. Being the only one who knew their genesis, Nat suggested that before dinner they meet in Nat's office to "do a little catching up."

Their catching up started with the three brothers peering intently into the large wall mirror in Nat's bathroom, trying to discern how they differed from one another. To their astonishment, they discovered that they did not differ vastly in any area, their clothes being where they most diverged, not in taste but in price. Buddy, who had inherited a toy company from his adoptive father, Hans Keebler, wore a hand-tailored blue mohair suit. Morton, who was a salaried law clerk for the British Home Office, wore a ready-made blue serge suit. Nat, the novelist, wore navy blue slacks and a navy blue cardigan ordered from a Neiman Marcus catalogue. It tickled them all to learn that blue was their favorite color. None of them had lost any of their teeth or their thick, wavy black hair, and even though their barbers lived thousands of miles from one another, the cuts were almost identical, short and neat. All three adored their adoptive parents, and only Nat, who had met Grimshade, knew how lucky they were.

The brothers compared scars and found that both Nat and Buddy had fallen going up a flight of stairs and had scars in exactly the same places on their chins. All had had their tonsils out by the time they were seven, and both Nat and Buddy had broken their right arms, Nat when he fell off a bike and

Buddy when he tried out a new pogo stick being developed at his father's factory.

"I sprained my right wrist twice," Morton quipped. "Does that get me into the broken-bone club?"

The timbre of their voices was eerily similar, Morton's differing mainly because of his British accent.

"It's a bummer," Morton complained jokingly. "I feel excluded — you two blokes have your broken arms and chin scars — and your quaint but faulty pronunciation."

Without missing a beat, Buddy and Nat simultaneously mimicked Morton's accent, Nat saying, "I feel excluded — it's a bummer," and Buddy saying, "You two blokes have your broken arms."

This eerie, unplanned exchange made them burst out laughing. Nat stopped and looked at his two happy brothers and decided to ask the burning question.

"Hey, guys, I have to know something. I talk to myself — a lot — and most times I don't know that I do. My wife keeps telling me that I do. I catch myself once in a while, but usually it's someone other than me who catches me, and it's embarrassing, to say the least. Do you guys — ?"

"That is so very strange," Morton interrupted, shaking his head.

"I know. That's why I'm seeing a shrink," Nat admitted. "Do either of you ever say aloud the things you're thinking?"

"Never," Morton answered. "But I do sometimes move my lips when I think. My wife, Sarah, says it's very unattractive. She says it looks like I'm cursing her under my breath. I don't know why I do it, but I've been at it since I can remember."

"I do neither of those," Buddy chimed in, "but I do a lot of humming — nonstop humming. Most times I am unaware that I am humming until someone joins me and hums along."

"It seems to me," Morton volunteered, "that all our idiosyncracies are motivated by degrees of discomfort."

"Discomfort about what?" Buddy asked.

"About being alone," Morton and Nat answered in unison.

"I think that may be it," Buddy concurred. "Well, we seem to agree about that."

As the triplets continued chatting, they found that they were in agreement about most things. All preferred soft scrambled eggs to fried eggs, all shaved with an electric razor, all were leg men — preferring to check out a woman's legs before assessing her bosom — none belonged to or attended a church, all enjoyed Emma Thompson's work in film, all liked dogs and tolerated cats, and all felt strongly that the planet was in deep trouble. Nat thought that segueing from the terrible state of the earth to the disquieting things he had learned in Boston and Houston about their birth parents was quite fitting. He didn't relish the thought of telling his brothers that Gelliard Grimshade, the man who had sired them, was a monster who had impregnated their mother, butchered her corpse by surgically removing three babies from her womb, and then sold them separately to three wealthy, childless couples. When Nat finished recounting the tale of horror, his brothers had the same reaction he'd had. They wanted to strangle Grimshade and decried the fact that he had committed suicide.

"Bastard denied us the pleasure of choking the life out of him!" was how Morton Quigley put it.

To a man, they agreed that it was unnecessary to pass on any of the horrific details to their loved ones. Morton and Buddy agreed that their newly discovered racial mix was completely unexpected, and neither found it unwelcome. They thought it incredible that Nat's favorite author as a kid was also theirs. They roared and clapped one another on the back when they discovered that Dumas's *The Count of Monte Cristo* was their all-time favorite story of revenge.

While Nat, Morton, and Buddy were learning about one another and trying to accept how weird it was to have two strangers using your face, Gertrude and Laylah were telling Glennie about their days at Creedmore and how Buddy had broken both their hearts. Gertrude, who still had strong feelings for Buddy, acted the perfect lady and graciously withheld the truth from everyone but herself. Seeing Buddy and Laylah together, she dared not allow herself to yearn for Buddy any longer. It was embarrassing for Gertrude to admit to herself that she was having similar yearnings for Nat and Morton. She'd been aware from the moment she met Nat that she had feelings for him and sensed he was attracted to her. She wondered how difficult it was for women married to twins and triplets to resist getting involved with their brothers-in-law.

When getting ready for bed that night, Glennie asked Nat, who had been strangely silent since the noisy hug fest and digital photo taking ended in their driveway, how he felt about the evening.

"On a scale of one to ten, honey, what do you think?"

"On a scale of one to ten" — he sighed — "I'd say an eleven and a half, a half higher than Nigel Tufnel — that guy in *Spinal Tap*!"

"I might even go to twelve," Glennie said, slipping a nightgown over her head.

"Glennie, I was wondering — when you saw the three of us together — what did you think — or rather, what did you feel?"

"I'm not sure I understand what you mean. What did I feel — about you and your brothers? I felt wonderful — oh, wait, you want to know if I felt an attraction to your brothers. Well, I've always liked the way you were put together — how your head sits on your square shoulders — your swarthy skin and your straight back — and your oh so original eye colors. I guess if I weren't married and y'all weren't spoken for, I'd get in the hunt again and try to bag one of you."

She laughed, threw her arms around him, and kissed his nose. "But I'd go after you first, because you are more interesting and the teeniest bit handsomer than those two — and besides, as far as I'm concerned, you are the original, so why settle for a copy. Hey, Nat, are you ready to make love to me or should I keep talking?"

"Talk dirty and we can do both," he said, nuzzling her neck as he pushed her gently onto their bed.

23

The week after Morton and Buddy returned home, the brothers had phoned one another every day, but now, a month later, they were down to a more sensible biweekly call. Eerily, without arranging it, they managed to alternate initiating the calls. Occasionally, when one of the brothers had something he felt would be of particular interest, he would arrange for a conference call. Today Nat placed that call.

"Buddy, Morton," he said, clutching two newspapers, "before I ask you how you are, I want to apologize. What happened is, this publicist who works for my publisher was visiting and saw those great photos Glennie took of us, and he asked for one. We should have known what he was going to do with it — but we weren't thinking, and —"

"— and he put that bloody photo of us in the newspaper!" Morton scolded. "It was in this morning's *Daily Mail*."

"And the *El Ahram* in Cairo!" Buddy said, feigning anger. "Where did you see it, Nat?"

"I saw it in two papers," Nat answered. "The *Los Angeles Times* and the *Daily News*."

"And the *International Herald Tribune*," Buddy and Morton announced in unison.

Before Nat could mount an apology, his brothers were laughing and commenting about their newfound celebrity.

"At last" — Morton chortled — "I'm finally getting my long-overdue fifteen minutes of fame!"

"A worker at our factory said to me, 'Mr. Keebler, I defended you when someone called you two-faced, but three-faced I cannot defend'!"

They all agreed that they were happy to share their unique story with the world. Buddy suggested the news story might inspire other adopted people to go out and find long-lost siblings.

"Right," Nat concurred. "And if nothing else, it makes for very enjoyable toilet reading."

Nat was not certain Dr. Frucht found the article and photo enjoyable, but he did detect a suppressed smile on the doctor's face when he handed back the news clippings.

"How do you feel, Mr. Noland, seeing

your picture in newspapers all over the world?"

"Great! Crassly speaking, Doctor, it won't hurt book sales. My publisher wants to schedule *NNNNN* for Christmas. What do you think?"

"What do *you* think, Mr. Noland? Do you think *NNNNN* is suitable for Christmas, considering the subject matter?"

"I hear you, Doctor — well, maybe not Christmas, but books sell well at holidays."

"Have you considered Halloween, Mr. Noland?"

Had he not detected the mischievous twinkle in the doctor's eye, Nat might have taken umbrage, but there would be no umbrage taken today — not during his farewell visit to the good doctor's office. Nat could never thank the doctor enough for encouraging him to search out his birth parents. Since reuniting with his brothers and having Dr. Frucht help him to wrestle with his demons, Nat had found relative peace. He rarely carried on conversations with himself without being aware of it.

And he was not sure how or why it had happened, but since the night of the grand reunion, he no longer balked at the idea of Glennie becoming pregnant. He shocked his wife that night by scorning the use of a condom, and the next morning he made her laugh when he handed her his stash of condoms to donate to "underprivileged horny teenagers, or to the neighborhood brothel."

When the session was over, Dr. Frucht did something that Nat had not seen him do before: walk with him to the hall door. There, the doctor surprised him again by offering an opinion.

"Mr. Noland," he said softly, "I would not be concerned about what you think was left unsaid by Mr. Grimshade. Whatever it is, it will come when it will come, and you will know of it. And if it never comes, that will be all right, too. Good-bye, Mr. Noland."

Nat hesitated at the door and listened to Dr. Frucht's receding footsteps. He thought of dropping in on Dr. Trampleasure, but he really had nothing to say to her. He had spoken to her the previous night when she called about seeing their photo in the *Los Angeles Times.*

"What a wonderful, wonderful photograph of you and Morton and Buddy. You all looked so happy, laughing and hugging each other so sweetly, it made me cry — with happiness," she added quickly. "I am so, so happy for all of you!"

As I and my brothers are so un*happy for*

you, was Nat's unspoken thought as they said good-bye and promised to talk again soon.

From the moment he turned on the ignition, and during the forty-minute drive home, Nat thought about Gertrude Trampleasure and how he might bring a little happiness into her life. He entertained the idea of Googling up a date for her on the Internet, but he quickly ruled that out. By the time he pulled into his driveway, he had come up with a fair idea.

After the festive Graduation from Dr. Frucht's Couch dinner that Glennie had prepared, Nat retired to his den and worked for a couple of hours at his computer before falling asleep at his desk. He awoke at seven the next morning, read over what he had written, corrected some punctuation, then rushed to the bedroom.

"Honey," he said, waking Glennie and handing her a page, "read this and tell me what you think!"

"I'll tell you what I think without reading anything. I think you're a stinker for waking me at — what time is it?" she asked, squinting at her watch.

"Almost noon," he lied. "Why don't you go pee — and then read this! I'll make you coffee and juice."

Glennie could never deny her husband anything when he was being cute and needy at the same time. She sat up in bed and read the page she was handed.

CIVVILIAA
A Multitude of Moons After the Byrth of Two Worthy in Nature Similar

As it must come to all males, so it came to the T.W.I.N.S. — the time of life when Kwigli and Keyblah must choose a mate to lie with — and make swell her belly. Kwigli had chosen Carilia, a sister to Eluria, who was large of buttocks, ample of bosom — and wide in her knowledge of the gathering and preparing of food.

For Neparia, all was well in Civviliaa, save for the sadness that befell her son Keyblah. With his T.W.I.N. now mated, Keyblah did feel alone and lost. Kwigli did offer to share his food and his wife with his brother, but Slama, the Leader, forbade it.

"As your father, Cain, did search out Neparia, who was not of his family, so must you. For witness what befalls a culture that is led by a man who chooses to beget with his own. Adam, closed of mind and heart, hath caused the Garden of Eden to wither and die."

Neparia did shed many tears when

Slama ordered that Keyblah venture forth in search of a maiden who would permit him to make swell her belly — and the population. The number who did inhabit Civviliaa had, worrisomely, remained at nine hundred and ninety-nine. Slama was impatient to add one more shiny black stone to the count.

For thirty-nine days and thirty-nine nights, Keyblah did search neighboring valleys for a maiden, but found none. On the fortieth night, Keyblah, asleep in a field of dandelions, did dream that he was lying with a chaste maiden, who, with her gentle hand, made swell his member. When he did awaken and behold a vision of loveliness beside him, he knew he had, indeed, been dreaming. When his member was rigidly erect, and he felt it being guided by the maiden's cool hand into the warmth of her body, did Keyblah know that it was a dream — a dream come true! And when their bodies were spent, Keyblah did say his name and she did smile, and she did say her name and Keyblah did smile, for he knew he had found the one whose body he would happily make swell many, many times. A most content Keyblah did fall to sleep that night, saying her name, Jertrudia — Jertrudia, over and over — and he did

awaken in the morning, whispering,
"Jertrudia, Jertrudia —"

"Jertrudia and Keyblah?" Glennie said, shaking her head. "Really, Nat! You are an incurable romantic!"

"It's the only thing I could think to do for her. I know it doesn't help her, but it makes *me* feel a lot better. Maybe it will give her a laugh."

"Or an ache. You're not going to tell Gertrude you used her name in your book, are you?"

"I will, after it's published," Nat said, taking the page from her, "and I'm hoping that, by then, she and her husband will find it amusing."

24

Paris

Since his divorce from Gertrude Trampleasure, Lars Lolafsen, who never under-
stood just how colossally boring he was, was
now on the last leg of a world tour, where he
had bored people of all nationalities on five
continents — but never Laura, who found
her husband fascinating and witty. When
the Lolafsens decided to have their breakfast at an outdoor café in Montmartre, they
could not foresee how, in a flash, the life and
fortunes of the gentleman who was seated
opposite them would be changed forever,
and how, in a peripheral way, Laura would
be the catalyst.

The Lolafsens, in order to collect interesting data to use in conversation with
people they encountered in their travels, always sat quietly during breakfast and
scanned their *International Herald Tribune*s.
They always bought two. Lars was the first
to notice the photo on the back page and its
headline, TRIPLETS REUNITED AFTER

FORTY-ONE YEARS. Lars, saying, "What an amazing photo!," sent Laura to the back page of her copy to see what he was talking about.

Lars had discovered the amazing photo, but it was Laura who uncovered the amazing story — and it was sitting just ten feet from them. Laura, a faster reader than Lars, finished the article first and looked up to catch the eye of the man at the next table. He was studying her, which was not unusual, for Laura often drew admiring glances, but when Laura sneaked a second look at the man, her mouth fell open, exposing the bite of brioche she had just taken. Without taking her eyes off the embarrassed gentleman, Laura nudged Lars, swallowed the bit of brioche, and walked over to the man.

"Sir, did you see *this?*" she asked excitedly, tapping the photo. "This photo? *Look at it, sir!*"

The frightened man, who was making his first trip back to Paris in twenty years, did as he was told. He looked at the photo and blinked, then looked up at Laura, then back at the photo, then blinked again. Soon everyone in the café was comparing the faces of the triplets in the photo to the face of the thunderstruck man who was mumbling,

"Impossible — impossible." As soon as he was able to compose himself, the man identified himself as Dr. Selwyn Green, then took out his cell phone and called the local office of the *Herald Tribune* and then his mother in Guatemala.

The *Tribune* editors, who sensed an even bigger human-interest story developing, assured Dr. Green that they would help him contact his brothers. Dr. Green's mother, who had seen the photo earlier that day and had been trying frantically to reach him, now, between sobs, told her son how she had lived her whole life in fear of this day — the day she would have to tell him the truth about herself — which she promised to do as soon as she could stop sobbing.

While the drama was swirling about him, Lars was staring intently at the photo. He was intrigued by the chin and earlobe of a woman whose identity was blocked by the shoulder of one of the triplets. By using his wife's stronger reading glasses, Lars was able to confirm that the earlobe, and the tiny diamond earring in it, belonged to someone he had known intimately.

That evening Gertrude Trampleasure was surprised to hear a phone message from her former husband — a message that was anything but boring. Lars started by saying that he had seen the photo of the reuniting triplets that featured "your lovely right ear-lobe wearing one of those exquisite Tiffany earrings I bought for you." On hearing how Lars and his wife had discovered Dr. Selwyn Green, whose DNA test would surely prove the triplets to be quadruplets, Gertrude went to her filing cabinet and plucked from it a folder labeled DR. J. J. FELLOWS BRACEBAHN. The folder contained dozens of scientific papers and essays about Dr. Bracebahn's innovative Institute of Applied Empathology. Gertrude was looking for a particular article that had been printed in the quarterly *Empathology Today.* She found the article and the name of the infuriating man who had commented negatively on a scientific paper that she had written.

"Well, well, Dr. Selwyn Green," she said with a sigh, scanning his article, "you may look like Buddy Keebler, but you reason like an ass!"

25

Dr. Selwyn Green dialed his mother's number, hoping that she had calmed herself sufficiently to tell him why she had lived in fear of this day all her life. He had always suspected that there was something more mysterious about his birth than being born out of wedlock. He had never fully accepted the story that his father was a bigamist and a Green Beret and had died in Vietnam. His mother claimed to have destroyed all photos of him because, as she said, "I don't want to look at the man who ruined my life and would have ruined yours!" Selwyn never believed that he had no living relatives in the world but his mother and his aunt Deborah, with whom she was currently living. He knew now that, at the very least, he had three very close kin.

At long last, a tearful Coretta Green was finally able to shed the guilt she had been carrying for too long. Selwyn, whom Coretta had raised as her son, was a man whose true identity she had not known until she saw his photo in the paper. She still had no knowledge of Gelliard Grimshade or his unsavory involvement in the conception and birth of her son and his brothers, nor would she be privy to it until Selwyn learned it from his brother Nat and passed it on to her. Coretta could not know and therefore could not tell him how and why God had chosen her to find him in a Dumpster.

Or why, on that fateful night forty years ago, Dr. Grimshade at first thought he held the afterbirth of Lena's third baby in his hands when actually he was holding the tiny, almost lifeless body of a fourth sibling. With proper medical equipment, Grimshade might have revived it, but he preferred not to jeopardize the lives of three babies by expending effort on a lost cause. *Although,* he thought, *having another baby to sell might be worth a try.* On the way to the hospital, the decision was made for him — the tiny infant stopped breathing. No one could know exactly why Grimshade opted not to take the dead infant to the hospital. One can only surmise that it was fear of the law that propelled him to wrap the tiny body in newspaper and toss it into a Dumpster — a McDonald's Dumpster into which, minutes later, Coretta, a part-time McDonald's employee, would toss a bag of trash. She imagined she heard a baby crying, but of late, Coretta often imagined she'd heard a baby crying. She started to walk away, but then she realized that the cry was real — and it was coming from the Dumpster! Coretta crossed herself and said a prayer before climbing into the bin and retrieving the crying bundle of newspapers. Without stopping to think, she ran out into the road, flagged a car, and begged an elderly man to drive her and "my baby, my poor baby!" to an emergency room. Deborah, the nurse on duty, was surprised to see Coretta again — and carrying a crying baby. A month earlier, Deborah had assisted a distraught Coretta in giving birth to a full-term seven-pound stillborn.

"I found him in a trash bin," Coretta explained tearfully. "It is God's will. *He* is giving me a second chance. The Lord wants me to care for this baby and raise him and love him as my own! Please help us."

Deborah knew that Coretta would be a better mother than the felon who had tossed the baby into the garbage, and she realized that if she admitted Coretta to the hospital, there would be no chance of her keeping the foundling. So, defying reason, ignoring hospital rules and legal consequences, Deborah spirited Coretta and the baby out of the emergency room and into her home, where she cared for little Selwyn until he was strong enough to accompany his new mother to Guatemala.

26

After fielding dozens of requests for exclusive photos and interviews with the quadruplets, Nat Noland thought it a good idea to meet with his brothers and their extended families to discuss how much of their private lives they wished to share with *The New York Times*, the *International Herald Tribune*, *USA Today*, *People* magazine, FOX News, *Vanity Fair*, *Reader's Digest*, and the *National Enquirer*. To this end, Nat and Buddy Keebler, who were the most financially able, secured airline tickets and hotel accommodations so they all could attend a family dinner in New York — the brothers, their families, their adoptive parents, their maternal grandfather, John Lomax, and members of his family.

"I am hoping," Nat wrote to each invitee, "that we will be able to help one another fill in the missing parts of our personal jigsaw puzzles — and have some fun in the process."

It was at the Plaza hotel, where Selwyn

Green, who was registered, and Gertrude Trampleasure, who was not, met by accident. Gertrude, who had checked in to the Sherry-Netherland, the venerable hotel diagonally across the street from the Plaza, was uncomfortable about meeting a man who looked exactly like a man who once adored her but was actually a stranger who had trashed her scholarly essay in *Empathology Today*. She was aware that Selwyn Green had no idea what she looked like and was concerned that he might find her as personally off-putting as he had found her essay.

Later that day, at the dinner party, when Gertrude told Nat of the unusual first meeting she and Selwyn had at the Plaza, Nat laughed and asked her permission to use it in one of his future novels.

"I'm a sucker for those couples-meeting-cute scenes in the old film comedies," Nat admitted. "And your cute meeting really — to borrow a phrase I used in my analysis — 'takes the cake'!"

That fateful afternoon at the Plaza, Selwyn was crossing the lobby on his way to the Oak Room when he fell in step behind a tall, graceful redheaded woman whose legs he found to be the two most attractive features he had seen since arriving in New

York. He was pleased to see her enter the Oak Room and considered introducing himself but reconsidered when he saw her being greeted warmly by a portly, gray-haired gentleman who he later learned was Dr. J. J. Fellows Bracebahn, the noted empathologist. The portly gent escorted Gertrude to a corner table, where they joined two young colleagues. The maître d' ushered Selwyn to a table that offered him an unobstructed view of Gertrude's back, which he welcomed.

Selwyn spent the next half hour splitting his attention between the editorial pages of *The New York Times* and the silky red hair that brushed the bare shoulders of the intriguing woman whose face he was most eager to see. When a three-tiered platter of tea sandwiches arrived at her table and he saw her reach for one, he actually heard himself say to a waiter the now classic line from the film *When Harry Met Sally*: "I'll have what she's having."

When she turned her head to bite into the tiny sandwich, Selwyn caught a glimpse of her extraordinary profile. This quick look did much to fortify his opinion that he was ogling someone well worth ogling. He watched her munch on a watercress sand-wich as the portly gent went about gormandizing most of the remaining sandwiches on the three tiers.

"These dainty teatime snacks don't go far," the gourmand muttered as he chewed. "Shall I order another tray of sandwiches? I believe that I've had my fair share —"

"And *my* fair share and *our fair lady's* fair share," his young colleague quipped.

"Our fair lady's fair share!" the portly gent repeated, roaring with laughter.

At the time, Selwyn could not have known that the pivotal factor in his meeting Gertrude would be the overeater's explosive reaction to a lame joke. The portly gent, who was laughing heartily and eating lustily, suddenly started choking seriously and gasping for air. It was apparent that unless someone acted, the man would choke to death. Dr. Selwyn Green, who in his fourteen years as the chief medical officer of hospitals in Kenya and Mali had handled every known medical emergency, rushed to the stricken man and executed a textbook Heimlich maneuver. What popped out of the portly gent was not strictly "textbook." The plug of compacted turkey, cheese, and watercress sandwiches was, but not the unexpected gusher of the undigested meatballs and spaghetti puttanesca that he had eaten for lunch.

Gertrude, who stood by ready to assist, was rewarded for her concern by being showered with the lion's share of her mentor's regurgitated Italian cuisine. Very little of her lovely silk dress was left unsplattered, and whatever the projectile vomiter had left in him he threw up on the lap of his now nauseated young woman guest, who, in turn, let fly a mushy glob of tea and petits fours all over Gertrude's new black leather pumps. Given the circumstances and the players, even a master dramatist could not have staged a more tragicomic encounter — or a more fortuitous one for Gertrude and Selwyn. Gertrude was not registered at the Plaza, and of necessity had to accept Selwyn's gracious offer to use his room to get out of her smelly dress and into a hot shower.

In the two hours they waited for the valet service to dry-clean her dress and polish her shoes, the two doctors talked and learned how very little they agreed upon in the matter of science but how little that mattered. What did matter was how the ordinary things, like a beautiful sunset, a visit to an art gallery, a Mozart quartet, projectile vomiting, or a hot shower, have the power to transform people's lives.

In their hearts, they both knew that the invigorating hot shower they were sharing at the moment would be but the first of many, long, hot, soapy showers they would take together in the years to come.

27

Nat Noland had done his share of television interviews and was always a little nervous before going on, but this afternoon, waiting in the studio's greenroom, his normal nervousness included a rapid heartbeat and sweaty palms.

He picked up his complimentary LARRY KING LIVE coffee mug and started to refill it.

Hey, schmucko, Nat's inner voice warned, *three cups of coffee in fifteen minutes is not a good idea!*

Yeah, you're right, Nat agreed, putting down his cup. *Just trying to stay awake for the next hour.*

Drink that and you'll be awake for the next month.

With Dr. Frucht's help, for almost a year Nat had not given voice to his thoughts in public. He did, however, continue to have full-voiced discussions during his writing sessions — and with Dr. Frucht's blessings.

"I see no good reason," the doctor advised, "to break up a winning team."

Nat had never been interviewed by Larry King, but he appreciated what a good interviewer the man was and, more important, what an appearance on *Larry King Live* might mean for sales of his new book. Nat could not believe that the book was finally in print.

To accommodate the number of friends and relatives who wanted to be present for today's unusual interview, Larry King had chosen to do the show in a small theater. In his introduction, Larry graciously mentioned all the books Nat Noland had written, and agreed with those people who found *Nadesjda* to be their favorite.

"Nat," Larry began, "your latest book, which I have read and, I must say, is remarkably different from anything you've written before — and, by the way, I loved it."

Just hearing that one compliment dried Nat's wet palms and slowed his heart rate. He managed a modest "Why, thank you, Larry."

"You're welcome, Nat. Say, before we talk about your new book, I wanted to ask you about that last book of yours. It started out as a . . . what?"

"Actually, it turned out to be a 'what,' "

Nat joked. "When I started it, I thought it would be a novel. Then when I was at the halfway point, I decided it would be a novella, and as I kept writing, I realized that the book would be less than a hundred pages, which was more like a novelette — and a sixty-page novelette is what I turned in to my publisher."

"And your publisher turned it into a —"

"— a thirty-seven-page, G-rated, illustrated, young adult book!"

Larry laughed. "So *NNNNN* started out as a novel and ended up as *Neparia*, a beautifully illustrated kids' book."

"Beloved by some kids but despised by adults of all ages — at least adults who preferred the Saint James version of Genesis to the Nat Noland version."

"It did stir up a bit of controversy."

"Not enough. I should have left in the sexy stuff."

"Well, let's get to your new work, Nat, and unlike your novelette, this is a biggie!" Larry said, displaying the book.

"Eight hundred and forty pages," Nat boasted.

"I'm not talking pagewise, Nat, I'm talking importantwise and saleswise. It's really something. I'd like to read this first page here, may I?"

"You said 'may I,' so of course you may," Nat quipped nervously.

Larry King turned to the title page and read," 'Good Jeans Trump Bad Genes: The Story of the Grimshade Quads, by Nat Noland.'

" 'This book is respectfully dedicated to the loving memory of a dishonest, unscrupulous, philandering, unprincipled, duplicitous, and detestable inhuman being — my father, Dr. Gilliard Grimshade.'

" 'The publication of this book was made possible by a touching and unexpected mandate from my three brothers, Buddy Keebler, Morton Quigley, and Selwyn Green; their wives, Laylah, Sarah, and Gertrude; my wife, Glennie; and my maternal grandfather, John Lomax. It was they who insisted that I write a detailed, warts-and-all-biography of the lives and times of the Grimshade quadruplets.' "

"Nat," Larry said, "I read the book so I know why you *respectfully* dedicated this book to a detestable human being, but explain it to our viewers."

"Well, Larry, besides being all those horrible things I outlined, he was other things, too, like a tremendously gifted, unlicensed obstetrical surgeon, and, for whatever his motive, Gelliard Grimshade placed my brothers and me into the hands of three great couples who turned out to be loving parents. We have to thank him for that."

"You write very touchingly about all of the parents," Larry said, picking up the book. "And by the way, Nat, in *Variety* this morning, I read that Warner Bros. has optioned the book."

"Yes. I read that too."

"It's a great role for a star — actually four great roles. So, Nat, who would be your first choice to play the quadruplets?"

"Larry, my first choice would be George Clooney or Jim Carrey or Robert Downey, Jr."

"Great first choices. Have you approached any of them?"

"No, Larry, but if I can have a close-up, I can approach them right now!"

"You got it! Close-up on Mr. Noland," Larry King ordered. "You're on, Nat."

"Messrs. Clooney, Carrey, and Downey," Nat said, looking straight into the camera, "if any of you are free from January to April of next year, how would you like to star in the film version of *Good Jeans Trump Bad Genes*?"

"Well, this is a first." Larry laughed. "Casting by cable. Now, about that title,

Good Jeans Trump Bad Genes — would you explain it?"

"Well, *Good Jeans,* the jeans with a *j,* represents the things parents choose to do for their kids, like loving them, paying attention to their emotional needs, feeding them, and buying them toys and books — and clothes, like a pair of blue jeans. The *Bad Genes* refer to the genes with a *g,* those genes a baby inherits. Research has shown that bad genes can be trumped by loving parents giving their adopted kids the time, care, and nurturing they need."

"Interesting theory."

"No theory, Larry! Living proof is looking right at you," Nat said, leaning across the desk and smiling into Larry's face.

"I hear you. And coming right at you, Nathaniel Noland," Larry said with a twinkle in his eye, "are three more living proofs. And what do you know, they're wearing their good jeans."

Larry and his staff had planned to surprise Nat, and he was that, as were the millions of viewers who were seeing the first national television appearance of the now famous Grimshade quadruplets. To both Larry's and Nat's surprise, the three brothers helped a resistant Nat out of his slacks and into the pair of designer blue jeans they had brought for him. Nat's strong bare legs came in for a healthy round of applause and hooting. The hooting stopped and the applause built when Larry King announced that the parents of these four men were seated in the audience.

"Say hello to the people who bought the blue jeans for these guys," he began. "From London, England, we have Morton Quigley's parents, Terrence and Sandra; from Carefree, Arizona, Nat Noland's parents, Jed and Bertha. All the way from Cairo, Egypt, Bernard Keebler's mother, Julane; from Guatemala, Dr. Selwyn Green's mother, Coretta; and from Houston, the boys' maternal grandfather, John Lomax. Oh, by the way," Larry added, "I am told that the boys' wonderful parents were amazed to discover that their child was not, as they had always boasted, the single handsomest boy in the world."

Larry then asked Nat's brothers, "So, how do you guys feel about the book and all the personal information in it?"

Morton and Buddy agreed that they were happy with the book, but Selwyn and, surprisingly, Nat were not pleased.

"Selwyn and I are sorry the book is out now," Nat explained. "We both have some stuff we would love to have included."

"What kind of stuff?" Larry asked.

"Oh, stuff like," Nat said offhandedly, "the names of the twin girls that Selwyn and Gertrude are expecting in about six weeks."

"And the names" — Selwyn shouted over the audience's applause — "the names of the twin girls Glennie and my brother Nat were expecting yesterday!"

28

Grace and Greta Noland, each weighing in at five pounds, one ounce, were born the night after Nat's appearance on *Larry King Live* — and the babies Gina and Georgia Green, each weighing four pounds, seven ounces, were born five weeks later.

Since the birth of the four girls, Nat had thought many times of his father.

I wonder what old Grimshade would say if he knew he had two sets of grand-daughters named for him.

He'd say, "Split them up and I can get fifty thou a pop!"

No, he'd say, "I can get two hundred thou if you don't split 'em!"

"Nat, enough trashing Dad — let's go to work."

"What are we working on?" he asked, looking at the blank computer screen.

"The screenplay, as soon as someone asks us to."

"What do we do in the meantime?"

"We could go to the nursery and play

with Grace and Greta."

"We just did."

"They might like a bath."

Nat helped Glennie bathe the twins and, after singing them to sleep, returned to the computer and wrote:

Grace and Greta, Greta and Grace,
Which do you think has the lovelier face?

Greta and Grace, Grace and Greta,
Which of the two do you like betta?

How do we choose one or the other?
Daddy sure can't and neither can Mother.

"Whaddya think, Nattie — lyrics to a song — or something to delete?"

"Something to delete!"

"Done!"

"Whoa, Nattie boy," he said. "Before you shut down, I have an idea."

"Type it out!" he ordered.

Nora Nadlinger had not ventured out of her apartment for seven months, so it was not surprising that she would be apprehensive about going to dinner with a man she had never met.

"Like it?"
"Well enough to try one more sentence."

All that Nora knew about Derek Noonan she had learned from the letters he had written to her while she was in prison.

Nat Noland smiled and said, "Let's see where this goes."
He put the cursor at the top of the page and typed:

★★★

NNNNNN
A new novel
by
Nat Noland

★★★

About the Author

Carl Reiner is a legend in the history of American comedy. Known primarily for his work as creator, writer, and producer of *The Dick Van Dyke Show*, he is also renowned as a comedian, actor, novelist, and film director. From his early work in the "Golden Age" of television, as an actor on Sid Caesar's *Your Show of Shows*, to his later film work with Steve Martin as the director of, among others, *The Jerk*, *Dead Men Don't Wear Plaid*, and *All of Me*, the twelve-time Emmy Award–winning Reiner has influenced three generations of American comedy.

Mr. Reiner recently appeared in *Oceans 11* and *Oceans 12*. He has written two semiautobiographical novels, *Enter Laughing* and *Continue Laughing*; two children's books (one cowritten with Mel Brooks); a book of short stories; a romance novel entitled *All Kinds of Love*; and a memoir entitled *My Anecdotal Life*. In 1999 the Academy of Television Arts and Sciences inducted him into the Television Hall of Fame, and in October 2000 he received the Kennedy Center Mark Twain Prize for American Humor. He lives in Beverly Hills, California.

13